HARD DAYS

Reuben Cole Westerns Book 3

STUART G. YATES

*For Janice
and my long-lost friend Norm, who was such a fan
of Westerns. Wherever you are, this one is for you.*

CHAPTER ONE

Apaches

They brought them in, four men, bound, heads bowed as they traipsed through the fort gates. Apaches. None turned and reacted to the many derisory comments and sneers from the civilians lining up to watch them. Some of the cavalrymen who formed the prisoner detail laughed. Cole threw a sharp glance at the officer in charge. "Shut your men up, Lieutenant!"

The young man turned away, shame-faced, and barked orders at his men. Disgruntled, the soldiers gradually fell into silence, but their scathing looks continued.

Riding alongside Cole, the young trooper who had gone out into the plains to track down the motley looking Indians, leaned closer. "Mr Cole, I'm not sure we should antagonise any of my fellow-soldiers. If we hint at any sympathy for these here savages, then I'm likely to come up against some bad feelings in the bunkhouse later on."

"Sympathy?" Cole's eyes grew dark. "These boys were ripped from their homes and forced marched across a hundred miles of scrub to a reservation that bears no resemblance to anything they have known. I don't blame 'em for breaking out. But shooting the guards, that was wrong."

"And that's why they'll hang."

1

"I believe so if it can be proved."

"Which it will be, surely."

"Unless hatred and suspicion get in the way. We have to be certain because if we ain't then there could be trouble. There are still roaming bands of Kiowa and Comanche out there and I hate to think what they might do if we act too hastily. Besides," Cole turned in his saddle and peered at the three Apaches shuffling bare-footed across the ground, "we didn't catch 'em all. There's at least two more out there."

"Including their leader perhaps?"

Grunting, Cole studied the young soldier. "You did well out there, son. I'm impressed. What did you say your name was?"

"Vance," and he gave an involuntary salute. "I haven't long been in uniform, Mr Cole. Still learning on the job, as it were."

"Well, you sure learned a lot these last few days, that's for sure. Next time we're called out to track down anyone, I'll be asking for you."

Red-faced, Vance quickly looked away, but couldn't suppress a grin. "My, that is praise indeed. Thank you, Mr Cole."

"You sound educated, son. I wonder why an educated young man would want to seek out a life in the U.S. Cavalry, especially out here in this godforsaken land."

"Lots of reasons."

"Well, I won't press you none, but I'm grateful that you did, whatever the reasons." He smiled before pulling his horse away, gesturing to the other troopers flanking the captured Apaches. "Move 'em over to the jail boys and make sure they is bound up tight."

"They're not going anywheres," said a rough-looking corporal, laughing.

"Even so, you don't take any chances with boys like this."

As the Indians shuffled by, the lead warrior stopped and looked up towards Cole. "You are the one they call He Who Comes. To be captured by you is an honour." He turned his attention to the other soldiers. "But I tell you this. We shall not submit, and we will bring suffering down upon you." He looked again at Cole. "Even you, He Who Comes."

Remaining tight-lipped, Cole watched as the scrawny looking Apache were pushed and shoved towards the tiny blockhouse prison.

"What did he mean by that?" asked Vance, rubbing his chin, a deathly pallor falling over his face.

"I don't know but go tell that Lieutenant to double the guards tonight, Vance. Just to be on the safe side."

Saluting, Vance eased himself from his saddle, stretched out his back, and crossed the parade ground towards the slowly dispersing crowd of onlookers. After listening to what Vance had to say, the Lieutenant shot a vicious glance towards Cole, who nodded once before turning away, his unease growing.

CHAPTER TWO

Julia

That evening, she made stew and dumplings, piling up Sterling Roose's plate until it was almost overflowing. Cole, sitting opposite his good friend, laughed. "You reckon you can get all that down you, Sterling?"

"I reckon so," said the wiry looking Roose as he attacked the stew with gusto.

"My," said Julia, "seems to me you haven't eaten for some time, Sterling. You need feeding up."

Chuckling between mouthfuls, Roose reached for the nearby plate of bread rolls and tore one in half. "I guess you could say so," he said then dunked the bread into the gravy and slurped it down.

"Sterling's been helping out old Sheriff Perdew down in Paradise," said Cole, his eyes twinkling with mischief.

"Really?" Julia asked and sat back, dabbing at the corner of her mouth with a serviette. "Don't he feed you too well?"

"Usual potatoes and gravy."

"For every meal?"

Roose nodded without looking up. "Every meal."

"Sterling has his heart set on being a law-officer," put in Cole, most of his attention on the piece of meat he was sawing through.

4

"You're not happy in the Army, Sterling?"

"Some," said Roose. "But it ain't what it used to be."

"Is that right," drawled Cole.

"You know it ain't."

His face came up and for a moment the two friends stared at one another.

"What are you talking about?" Julia, noticing the charged atmosphere looked from one to the other. "Cole? What does he mean?"

Roose got in first. "The southern plains are all but tamed now. Within a year, maybe two at the most, even the Comanche will be in a reservation, but there are rumours of unrest in the north."

"What sort of unrest?"

"Sioux and Cheyenne," said Cole, victorious at last over the meat. He popped a large chunk into his mouth and chewed it down with some effort. "The great tribes of the Plains. They've just about had enough."

"But what has that to do with us down here?"

"Not a lot." Cole's face came up and caught Roose's cold stare. "Maybe."

Shifting uneasily in her chair, Julia's voice broke a little as she said, "You're scaring me."

"No, no," said Roose quickly, reaching out to pat her forearm. "No need to be scared. It might just … spread, that's all, so we have to be ready."

"Not that it's gonna happen," said Cole, his eyes settling on the way Roose's fingers gripped Julia's arm.

For the rest of the meal they ate in silence, the only sounds ones of cutlery against crockery, satisfied moans and smacking of lips. When finished, Julia gathered up the empty plates and took them into the tiny kitchen before returning with a stone jug. She poured out frothy beer into chipped cups before sitting down and gazing at the two men as they drank.

"So, tell me," she said. "Those Apaches you brought in? They will hang?"

"Almost certainly," said Roose, wiping his mouth and sitting back in

5

his hard-backed chair. Behind him the open fire crackled and spat, the stacked logs giving off an intense, yet comforting heat. "I reckon it's what they call 'an open-and-shut case' due to the survivors who will give testimony."

"I'm surprised such savages will be given a fair hearing."

"That's the law," put in Cole. He took a deep breath. "At least around here."

"That's down to you," said Roose, his voice flat. He gazed into his beer.

"Not only me," said Cole, shifting uncomfortably in his own chair.

Frowning, Julia looked from one to the other. "What does he mean, Reuben? Down to you? Down to you in what way?"

"He won't say so himself," put in Roose quickly, "but dear old Reuben here wrote to President Grant begging him to give his reassurance that Indians would be allowed due process."

"You wrote to the President?" Julia sat back, amazed.

Cole shrugged, "It was nothing," he said in a quiet, embarrassed voice.

"And what did the President say? Did he answer?"

"Not to me directly, but the fort received a communication, suggesting they proceed with caution. Trouble is brewing up north and the Government is anxious it doesn't spread."

"It will," said Roose, draining his cup, "no matter how we deal with incursions and the like down here."

"Incursions? Sterling, this is their land. They've lived here for thousands of years. We just charged right in and took what we wanted."

"Not me," said Roose, his jawline reddening. "I never posted no claim for gold or anything else for that matter."

"I didn't mean you personally, Sterling! You know that wasn't my meaning."

"Even so, gold is a mighty temptation, and them Indians have no use for it so what's the problem?" He produced a small canvas bag and set about rolling himself a cigarette.

"Ooh, just wait a moment," said Julia and jumped up to cross to the small dresser set against the wall next to the door. She came back with a small wooden chest, opened it, and produced two slim, black cheroots. "I got these from the store. Thought you might like one?" She handed it over to Roose who looked at it with wide-eyed relish.

"She ain't nothing but hospitable," said Cole, taking the cheroot Julia offered him and twirling it under his nose. "That smells mighty good, Julia."

"I thought I'd splash out, seeing as you are back safe and sound."

Having lit his cheroot, Roose leaned across and, cupping his hands to protect the match flame from a non-existent breeze, lit up Cole's also. "He does seem to do that with some regularity."

"Well," she reached out and squeezed Cole's arm, "it's good to have you here. There's a world of work to do and those horses could do with a run-out."

"I'll see to that in the morning." He caught her look and chuckled, "All right, *we* will see to it in the morning!"

They all laughed, and Julia seemed a little relieved. "I'll make coffee."

Watching her leave the room, Roose smiled as he puffed on his smoke. "She's beautiful."

"She is."

"And yet ..." He leaned in closer, lowering his voice. "If I may say so, old friend, you don't seem ... too set."

"That's because I'm not."

Roose frowned. "But I thought—"

"It was never my intention to have a relationship, Sterling. Nor hers, I reckon."

"I think you're wrong there, Cole. She's loyal, caring. Even devoted, you could say."

"My only thought was to protect her until such time as she feels able to move on."

"Are you kidding me? You'll never find another like her."

"You could be right, but I could never ask anyone to share my life right now, not the way things are. You know how dangerous it is out there."

"Yeah, but ... If she is willing to take the risk, to be with you, to make sure you don't do anything too stupid, why not allow yourself to—"

He stopped abruptly as the sound of approaching horses from beyond the front door made themselves heard.

Cole quickly pulled out the handgun from its holster hanging on the back of his chair just as Julia came rushing in, face ashen. "What is it?"

"I don't know," said Cole as Roose took down the Henry repeating rifle from the hooks above the door. "Cut the lights."

She did so, moving across to the large oil lamp on top of the dresser first. The one in the centre of their table followed, the only glow remaining was that coming from the kitchen.

The darkness seeped over them and Cole went to the shuttered window adjacent to the door and eased up the wooden bar. He peered into the night.

A voice called out, "Mr Cole? It's me, Hyrum Vance. We've got a problem back at the fort, sir."

Cole let his breath out long and slow. "All right, thanks." He turned away and if it wasn't for the dark, he felt sure he would see Julia wringing her hands, glaring at him.

CHAPTER THREE

Apache Breakout

On the ride back to the fort, Vance outlined what had happened. "Seems like the ones we didn't find came back, climbed the walls and broke into the jail." The wind lashed against them, forcing them to bend low over the necks of their horses. Vance was shouting to make himself heard, but Cole managed to get the gist of the story. Two guards had been knocked down, but not killed, a point not lost on the army scout. Even so, when they came into the parade ground, Captain Fleming was standing waiting, with a face like thunder. He hadn't had time to dress correctly and appeared somewhat comical in long-johns, riding boots and hat. Behind him, sprawled out in front of the jail, two troopers were being tended by a subaltern who cleaned their bleeding heads.

"You took your time," growled Fleming, holding onto Cole's horse as the scout dismounted.

"That's my fault, sir," said Vance quickly, stepping up beside them. "I rode out as fast as I could but got lost."

Fleming silenced him with a glowering look. "I'll settle you later, private. Right now, Cole, we have a situation. Come into my office."

Inside the cramped office, one of Fleming's men had stoked up the pig-stove in the corner and both captain and Cole pressed up close to it, warming their hands. "This is mighty welcome, Captain."

"This is only the onset of winter," said Fleming, "soon it'll feel like death."

"Maybe for those Apache too."

"I want them caught, Cole. All of 'em this time."

"I underestimated 'em," admitted Cole grudgingly. "I never expected the others to come here, least of all to attempt a breakout. They must be desperate."

"So they should be. They know the noose is waiting." Fleming shook his head. "Beats me why they didn't kill the guards. They are already as guilty as sin."

"Maybe they don't see it that way."

Fleming turned, his eyes colder than the night. "I've heard you muttering about savages before, Cole. Seems to me you're a little too soft on 'em."

"No, sir. I do not condone anything they have done; I just feel justice should be served in its proper manner."

"Same as us, you mean? Bull!" He turned away, his shoulders tense as the anger seized him. "I have fought them many times and the only justice they recognise is that delivered by a bullet. So, you get out there and bring 'em back. Dead or alive, I don't care which."

Cole turned to go without a word.

"You should take that other scout with you, to ensure success this time. What's his name, the scrawny one?"

"Sterling Roose, Cap'n. But no, I asked him to stay at my ranch, just in case."

"Just in case of what?"

"They know me. Who knows what they might do once the killin' starts ... which it will, I guess."

"Your heart ain't in this, is it Cole."

"From where I'm standing, I think those boys will try and make it down into Mexico and we'll never see 'em again. But if we start bringing down some wrath of God upon their heads, they may just repay us in kind."

"They killed a guard at the reservation. They must be brought in to face that."

"I wonder if we'd be so desperate to see justice served if the guard had been Kiowa."

Fleming blew out a breath. "Get out of here, Cole, I'm sick of your sanctimonious drivel. And, furthermore, I've decided I'm coming with you."

Cole's eyes widened. "To babysit me, Cap'n?"

"To make sure you do what is required, Cole. You're getting soft."

Stepping out into the night, Cole crossed to where Vance stood next to the horses. The young soldier brought himself stiffly to attention. "Are we setting out straight away, Mr Cole?"

"As soon as the good Captain is ready, yes."

"Oh." Vance looked over to the light burning in Fleming's office window. "I guess that means we'll be taking an entire troop with us. That'll take some time to prepare."

"Seems so, and the longer we delay the farther away those Apache get." He shook his head. "Julia ain't gonna be happy, I know that."

"Mr Cole," said Vance in a grim sounding voice, "ain't none of us gonna be happy."

CHAPTER FOUR

Arrival

It was in the late autumn of seventy-five, some three months before the Apache breakout, that a young man, tall and lean in the saddle, rode into the town of Paradise with murder on his mind. He tied his horse to the hitching rail outside the Parody Hotel and Saloon, kicked his dusty boots against the entrance steps and pushed his way through the batwing doors just as Sarah Lamprey was coming out. Looking flushed, all full-bosomed black dress and dark purple bonnet with matching parasol, she glared at the man, stopping him in his tracks.

"Afternoon, ma'am," he said, tipping his hat.

Ignoring him, Sarah Lamprey huffed and went into the street, the young man's eyes following her hour-glass figure.

"No point you thinking dark thoughts," said a voice. The young man turned to see a large, lurching man leaning against the swing doors, huge forearms looped over their top. He grinned. "She ain't the courting kind."

"I ain't even—"

"Ah shoot, of course you weren't." Grinning, he stepped back and pulled the doors open, gesturing for the young stranger to enter.

The stranger surveyed the interior, filled with men wrapped up in thick coats, hats and scarves, a brown fug rising from their collective bodies to mingle with the acrid smoke of numerous cigarettes, cigars, and pipes. Their many voices rumbled low, like the steady progress of a distant locomotive.

It wasn't long before he gained the information he required. A gregarious and good looking individual, his blond hair flopped over one of his crystal blue eyes, giving him a boyish look. Smooth chin, full lips and an aquiline nose contributed to his comely features. He knew well enough the effect he had on those to whom he spoke. Captivated, his audience warmed to him and put him in the direction of one or two possibilities.

Riding out to the 'Celestial Ranch' owned by Francis Rancine, a wealthy cattle rancher whose business was flourishing, the young man presented himself to the portly gentleman sat behind a vast table, eyes peering out from under thick, bushy eyes, studying and dissecting the stranger before he spoke. "I am looking for hands," he said, "but you don't look much like a cow-poke, son"

"No sir, I'm more of an odd-job person, mending and fixing and the like."

"Well, we have plenty of that work to do." He shot a glance towards his charge-hand whose scowling face told the young man that this was someone who would take some convincing.

"Please, all I'm asking is a chance. I'll work for free if that's what it will take."

"Seems you is desperate, son," said the big chargehand, his stare never faltering. "Maybe you is runnin' from something ... or someone."

"No, sir, it is not that at all. I just need a new start is all. I lost my ma and pa some six months ago and ... Well, to be honest, there are too many memories back in my hometown. I need to start again, build a new life for myself."

"So, there ain't no lawmen on your trail?"

"No, sir. I swear it, on my dearly departed momma's grave." To give credence to his words, he raised his right hand, "As God is my witness, I do not—"

"All right, son," cut in Rancine, "you don't have to give us any more explanations." He looked at the chargehand again, "Seems like a week's trial wouldn't go amiss here, Hank."

"I guess not," said Hank, sticking his thumbs into his belt, a belt which sported a tied-down Colt Peacemaker. "What did you say your name was, son?"

"Emmanuel Torrance," said the young man, "but most people just call me Manny."

"All righty, *Manny*. You follow me and we'll ride over to the bunkhouse. You can meet up with some of the boys later on."

Deep in thought, he lay on his bunk, arms behind his head, waiting for the sun to set, knowing that soon the cowboys would be returning from a long day out in the fields. With his eyes wide open he stared at the ceiling, the way the knotted tree trunks held up the roof, knowing this was a well-constructed building but that it would burn easily. If the time ever came when he would need to make his escape, burning this place down would be one way to disguise his departure. The cowhands would be so intent on putting out the blaze that he could disappear without fear of anyone pursuing him, at least not for a long time. Not that they'd know where he was going, or why. Hadn't Shapiro told him all would be fine? Didn't he trust Shapiro with his life? Of course, he did and as he lay on his bunk and stared upwards, his mind drifted back to when he met the man who offered him a way out of all his worries.

He stood and watched as they brought Sergeant Burroughs in. As silent as the dead, his eyes never flickered as they pulled him from the saddle, and he caught sight of Torrance standing only two or three paces away. Of course, he was Torrance only to the people of the Rancine ranch. His real name was Nolan, cavalry trooper, one of the soldiers Burroughs used to cover his own treasonable tracks. Stealing and selling Army horses, something he'd been doing for longer than anyone knew. To help, he'd enlisted an eclectic mix of partners – including Julia's husband. They were all dead. Most of them anyway. Except for Sergeant Burroughs who would face the hangman's noose for his efforts.

Except he didn't.

He'd escaped and Nolan, fearing for his life if he were implicated, had disappeared into the vast expanses of the Colorado/Utah territories. There he'd wander into small, half-deserted towns, as anonymous as himself. He changed his name and the veil fell over him, while every night he'd dream of her, Julia Rickman. He did not believe he had ever seen a woman as beautiful as she. Such thoughts made him feel somewhat better.

The days seemed endless and pitiless, however, until he met Shapiro and listened to his story before sharing his own of the man who had changed both their lives.

CHAPTER FIVE

Shapiro

I t started almost immediately on the day he left home. An easy decision, given that he'd just shot his father in the guts with the old man's Colt Paterson, a gun which he had inherited from his father who had served in the Texas navy in the old days. Now, as Vernon Shapiro lay dying on the cabin floor, his son stepped away, the smoking gun in a hand that shook uncontrollably. He felt a red-hot tear rolling down his face. It was to be the last time he cried.

Ever since he could remember, Paul Shapiro held nothing but fear and hatred for his father. It seemed to him that if he merely breathed at the wrong moment, the big old man would cuff him heavily across the ear. Beatings became something of a ritual whilst his mother watched and wailed but did nothing to halt the violence. Even now, as Vernon moaned, gripping the wound in his stomach, she stood in the door, wringing her hands, saying, "Oh my, Paulie ... Oh my ..."

After the killing, Paul Shapiro rode away without a glance and soon found himself in bad company, robbing stagecoaches together with a bunch of gormless young layabouts whose propensity for violence knew no bounds. The Rangers hunted them down mercilessly and only Paul and his friend Shamus O'Donnell managed to escape into the wild untamed New Mexico territory. That was before the War but, of course, that conflict was to change everything, certainly for everyone who served in it and survived.

For Shapiro, the War proved profitable beyond imaginings. Living on the outskirts of major towns, news filtered through to him slowly and shipments of weapons would always grab his attention and soon the Confederacy were making good use of his talents. He attacked Union Army supply wagons whenever he could, using a growing gang of vicious but resourceful men to help him in his endeavours.

It was during a lull in operations that everything changed for Shapiro. He and his band were resting up in a bordello on the Mexican border, drinking whisky and tequila, the real world far away from their minds or their cares. On the third morning, Wilf Penn stepped out onto the veranda and stretched his limbs, groaning with joy at the feel of the warm sun on his face. A bullet hit him in the head, and he fell like a stone, dead before he even knew what had happened.

As the others flung themselves out of their beds and their lethargy, a fusillade of bullets erupted through the thin, adobe walls, sending up clouds of white powder and shards of broken plaster to spatter against bare arms and bemused faces.

Screaming at his men to keep down, Shapiro, sweat-stained vest the only piece of clothing he wore, rushed out into the daylight, bent double, Colt Navy in his hand, loosing off wild, blind shots as he raced towards his horse. "Get out, boys," he screeched, chancing a look towards the nearby hillside and the black smudged outlines of men kneeling there. At least a dozen, possibly more. Army, some in green vests, and his stomach rolled over at the knowledge of who and what they were.

Sharpshooters. Men well drilled and talented in the use of their chosen weapon, the Sharps breech-loader. They must have been hunting him and his men for weeks. Now, they were here, and it didn't seem to Shapiro that they were about to take any prisoners.

To underline his thoughts, as he struggled to mount his horse, three of his men burst out from the bordello door, guns barking, and the sharpshooters on the hill took their aim and dropped each of them, several bullets slamming into each torso.

Cursing, Shapiro kicked at his horse and tried to move away. A figure stepped out, barring his way, dressed in frayed hunting shirt and knee-length boots. From under the wide brim of his hat, furious eyes gazed out, locking in on Shapiro as his shouted, "Hold up, boy. It's over."

Gawping, Shapiro threw back his head and laughed before bringing up his Colt in a blur, only to have it shot out of his hand.

"Don't be stupid," said the brown-shirted stranger, stepping up close to grip the reins, his own Navy smoking, "or I'll kill you in your saddle."

With no choice left, Shapiro, clutching at a hand ringing with pain, slid down to the ground and knelt groaning and trying his best to stem the flow of blood from his shattered fingers. "You smashed up my gun hand real good, you miserable bastard."

From nowhere, the stranger's fist cracked into his jaw and sent him reeling backwards. "Don't tempt me to shoot apart the other one, boy."

Shapiro blinked back tears. "I'll learn to shoot with my other hand and I'll kill you dead."

The stranger smiled. "If you live that long."

Closing his yes, Shapiro sucked in his pain and surrendered.

CHAPTER SIX

Nolan's Journal

It is true that without the help of Shapiro I would have ended up at the end of a noose or maybe even a bullet in the back. I'd lost my way, desperate for food and shelter, moving from one rotting gold-mining town to the next. My clothes were tattered, threadbare, and my horse, the only thing apart from my Henry rifle I owned, was suffering as much as I. In the last town I drifted into, the ostler at the saloon stables shook his head, a sad look in his eyes. "She ain't got long, young fella." He stroked her nose, peering into her eyes, and tutted. "Nah, not long at all. She's all broken down." His eyes narrowed as he studied me. "A little like you."

I put a knife in his throat, hid his body in one of the stable stalls and, taking whatever he had, saddled up a new mount and walked it outside. It was then I heard the gunfire.

It seemed the whole main street was alive with desperate men, six-guns barking, horses screaming. Townsfolk were there in numbers, some of them with ancient muzzle loaders, sending hot lead in the direction of a group of swarthy looking individuals bursting out of the tiny bank. The town of Grievance, I was to learn later, was well known for being the home of one of the most secure vaults in the whole territory. Those robbers were there to plunder its contents that much was clear, but for whatever reasons they were making a hard time of it. Two of them were already lying bleeding, maybe even dead, on the boardwalk. A couple more were running, bent double, towards their tethered horses whilst a third stood in the bank doorway, firing at anyone who came into his sights.

It was then I made the decision which was to change my life forever.

Throwing myself into the saddle, I spurred my new horse into the midst of the gunfight, my six gun in my hand, blazing away at the townsfolk and sending them scattering in every direction. They were not gunmen and they gave up their struggle without much trouble. Urging my horse on, I made it to the bank to see the man in the doorway staring at me, his eyes the blackest I have ever seen.

"Come on," cried one of his companions, struggling to keep control of not only the horse he straddled, but a second fiery stead, bucking and plunging as if seized by a fearful fit.

The man in the doorway gave me a look, holstered his gun, and raced into the street. A bank teller appeared behind him, sawn-off shotgun in both hands. He raised to discharge both barrels and I shot him through the chest, hurling him back into the bank. Keeping my own horse under control I watched the black-eyed robber hauling himself into the saddle. Again, the look, accompanied this time by the faintest of smiles. Then, whooping at the top of his voice, he broke into a gallop, his surviving gang close behind.

I followed, without hesitation.

We camped some hours later when we were certain any pursuers had long since given up the chase. The leader, as I learned who black-eyes was, introduced himself as Shapiro, the others as Mel, a young chancer from back east, and Olaf, a huge Norwegian bruiser who took an instant dislike to me. As we sat around the drinking coffee, he glared at me across the makeshift campfire until at last he could hold his patience no longer and burst out, "How come you sprang out of nowhere, puppy-dog, and shot all those people up? Who are you?"

"Steady Ol," said the younger Mel over the rim of his steaming coffee mug, "if it weren't for him, we'd be—"

"We'd be *what*? Dead?"

"More than likely."

"Well maybe that is what we will still be when he slits our throats in the night."

I stared at him. He was a massive hulk of a man, his hands like barn doors, the muscles in his neck fit to burst through his shirt collar. The thick coat he wore only served to accentuate his imposing size. "Why would I do that?" I demanded, not caring for his tone, nor his size. I was not afraid to mix it with anyone, despite having my head broken once or twice in the past.

"To claim the bounty, that's why."

"Are you crazy," cackled Mel, setting his coffee mug down. "He's as much wanted as we are after what he did."

"Perhaps more so."

It was the first time Shapiro had spoken since we found that place. Every head turned towards him. "For killing that bank teller, I am grateful, but I think you did yourself no favours."

"I wasn't looking for any."

"Then why'd you do it," snarled Olaf.

I shrugged, finishing my own coffee. "I'm in something of a fix, as you can see." I ran my hand over my tattered garments. "I ain't had a square meal for over a week and I'm just about run out of options."

"So, that's it?" The Norwegian said sceptically. He grinned, without humour. "You saw throwing in with us as a chance to better your situation? Nah, I don't believe it. You did what you did for what you could get out of it, and I don't like—"

"Olaf," said Shapiro, his voice low and thick with menace, "he saved our skin. Now you either accept that for what it is, or ..."

"Or what? You don't own me, Shapiro. If you ask me, I think you're blind to what this stranger is." He turned to me again, his eyes mere slits, his mouth a thin line. "A bounty hunter."

He went for his gun. It was an ill thought out move, sitting all hunched up, his bulk a hindrance to pulling his gun smoothly from its holster. Even as I made a grab for my gun in response, Shapiro was faster than either of us, and he shot Olaf between the eyes and ended the dispute there and then.

Squealing, Mel stood, hands raised, palms outstretched as he retreated away from the fire. "What in the hell? Shapiro, no. For pity's sake."

Shapiro put two bullets into him and as Mel fell dead to the ground, I sat there, rooted, not knowing if I was to be next. I held my breath as Shapiro turned his wild, black eyes towards me, his gun held rock still. "Drop it," he said.

I let my Colt fall from my trembling fingers and waited for my own end to come.

Instead of a heavy slug throwing me backwards, I saw him put his hand gently over the hammer and disengage it. I felt such a rush of relief I almost swooned. "Honesty," he said, his eyes never leaving mine, "is rare. By the look of you, I would say your story is a truthful one."

"It is, I swear it."

He held up his hand as he slipped his gun back into its holster. "I believe you. Unlike those two dogs," he nodded to the corpses of the others, "who would have slit my throat for a nickel. One of them sneaked out of camp two nights ago, thinking I had not noticed. I know now he went to warn the town about our attempt to rob the bank, get me killed then claim the bounty. If you hadn't stepped in when you did ..." He shook his head sadly. For a long time, he sat staring at the ground, lost in thought. I thought at one point he may have fallen asleep but then, just as I was about to say something, he sprang back into life and raised his head, eyes bright and alive once more. "Now, as we is to ride together, I want you to tell me all about yourself and why you are in such a state."

So, I told him everything, from joining the army to being drafted into Sergeant Burrough's troop. I told him how the order came to find the thieves who had stolen Army horses from farther north and were leading them down to the Mexican border in the hope of selling them. How Reuben Cole, the Army scout, had uncovered the fact that Burroughs was in on it and—

"*Wait*," hissed Shapiro, sitting bolt upright, a darkness descending his eyes, "Cole, you said?"

"Yes. He is an Army scout, assigned to our troop to aid us in tracking down the horse-thieves." I frowned. "You know him?"

"Oh yes," he snarled before turning his head to spit into the ground. "We have had dealings ..." Once more, he fell into a dark silence. Clearly something had passed between Cole and him, something bad.

Soon we rode away from that killing ground, taking the horses and whatever we needed from the bodies. We crossed the endless open range, never pausing for rest, drinking from our water canteens on the hoof. Shapiro, intent to put as much distance as he could between us and the town of Grievance, seemed like one possessed, and when we finally camped, he told me of his plan.

CHAPTER SEVEN
The Plan

There was nothing but hard, corn biscuits to eat, but they made a feast of it, relishing every mouthful, washing it all down with the last of their coffee.

"There is a bank in the town of Paradise," said Shapiro as he gulped down his final morsel. "It holds money from the railroad company. Every Thursday, armed men come to collect cash to pay the railroad workers' wages. One of my gang, a man called Arkan Lomas, worked as one of the guards. He told me of this. My hope was we could raid the bank on that day, take the money and head for Mexico. Cole put paid to all of that." He held up his hand, rotating it to reveal the livid scar running across the back of the wrist. "He shot my gun out of my hand. I've never known shooting like it."

Pursing his lips, Nolan nodded. "I saw him go up against Burroughs and his men. Ice cold and deadly."

"Yes." Shapiro studied the scar. "I thought I was good with a gun, until I came up against him."

"What happened to Arkan?"

"Dead, along with the rest but I can easily gather together another gang. There are plenty of desperate men to be found throughout the

Territories, former gold and silver miners, railroad workers, ex-army. You are not the only one to have fallen on hard times."

"So, your plan is to raid the bank in Paradise?"

"Yes. But it is not the money which drives me, although that will be bait enough for the men I recruit. No, it is Cole I want. And that is where you come in, my friend."

Nolan took a breath. "I don't see what I can do, other than telling you more about his capabilities."

"From what you have told me, you knew the woman, the one who double-crossed Burroughs, the one who escaped?"

"You're well informed, I'll say that."

"I always keep myself one-step ahead. So, you knew her?"

"Miss Julia? Well yes, I knew her, but only slightly."

"She will remember you."

"Maybe, but I don't see how I can—"

"It is simple, my friend. I want you to reacquaint yourself with her, make her your friend, your confidant."

"My what?"

Shapiro sighed. "Make her trust you. Perhaps even love you."

Nolan guffawed, "No way would she do that!"

"Maybe not your lover, but something close. I want her to betray Cole for you."

"Betray him? I don't understand."

"Do you think I have done nothing since I escaped from his clutches? I have sought him out many times, watching, listening, learning. I have even visited his ranch. An easy thing to do as he is hardly ever there. He and the woman, they share that ranch together now."

"So, she *is* his lover?" Shapiro nodded and Nolan appeared downcast, taking on a mournful expression, and shaking his head. "Then there is even less chance for me to wangle my way into her affections."

"No. I think there is every chance. He pays her no mind, leaves her to tend to his horses and land whilst he goes away on his scouting duties. She is alone and lonely." Smiling, he leaned forward, "Trust me on this, my friend. I know women, what they yearn for. You will have no problem in seducing her. You are young, handsome, and kind."

"That's hardly what I'd call myself," scoffed Nolan. "She is a sophisticated yet hard woman. She shot Burroughs without a thought."

"Because he had wronged her."

"Yes."

"As you will convince her Cole has also wronged her. Perhaps in a different way, but the outcome will be the same. Or almost."

"Do you ..." Nolan tipped back his hat and ran a hand through his hair. "Let me get this straight. You want me to convince Miss Julia that Cole is in some way cheating on her, causing her to find some comfort in my advances, then ... Then *what?*"

"Lure him in. I want her to confront him, tell him what has happened between you and her because of the way he has neglected her. He will be devastated, and his guard lowered. Then, at that precise moment, you and the others will hit the bank, and when news reaches him at his ranch, he will respond and prepare to return to town. I will be waiting, and I will kill him. He will be in no condition to defend himself due to his state of mind."

"That's a complicated plan, Shapiro."

"Maybe, but I think it will work. It all hinges on you, my friend. You will get a job at one of the bigger ranches and bide your time until you are able to make yourself known to her."

"How am I supposed to do that?"

"Find a way to make herself beholden to you so she will invite you to work on Cole's ranch. As the time passes, she will grow fond of you, I know it."

"You seem awfully sure of all this. How much time are you talking about?"

"As long as it takes. I have already waited almost years to have my revenge, I can wait a few months longer."

"A few months?"

"It must be natural, not forced. You will bring me reports of how you are progressing."

Nolan wandered a few paces away to stare out across the plains. The ground hard, unforgiving. The year was moving on and soon the weather would change, bringing with it cold and snow. No matter what the season this was a harsh, barren, and friendless land, not one for the weak of spirit.

Shapiro stepped up alongside him and rested a hand on the young man's shoulder. "You'll be well rewarded, my friend."

"It's not that I'm thinking about."

"Oh? What then?"

Nolan turned his face towards his companion. "Julia. What if ... What if the feelings develop into something real?"

"Then your reward will be greater than any monetary gain, my friend!" Shapiro laughed and slapped Nolan hard on the shoulder.

But Nolan did not return the man's laughter. Instead, he closed his eyes and took a huge, shuddering breath.

Shapiro stared at his new companion, his laughter drifting away. At that moment, he knew Cole would not be the only one to die when this plan came to its inevitable conclusion.

CHAPTER EIGHT

Cole

S everal months after Nolan's meeting with Shapiro the first flurries of snow fell, dusting the mountains with soft, white powder. From a distance an observer might think it romantic, wistful almost, the sort of view to turn one's mind to ideas of long winter evenings nestled in front of burning log fires, holding one's beloved close. Cole knew it was none of these things. Nature was turning, transforming the land from baked hard to one riddled with deep ruts hidden under the snow where untold perils could throw a horse, twist its ankle. After that, the chances of finding oneself exposed and alone, to suffer and freeze to death multiplied. Winter was the time Cole feared most. Its uncertainties, its unforgiving nature. Blazing sun he could cope with, prepare himself for, have enough water to get him through, but winter ... No, winter was another animal altogether. And it was not one he trusted.

Beside him, Captain Fleming stared up to the mountain peaks and sighed. "You think they would have come this way?"

"Could be," said Cole. He'd picked up the trail two days ago and hadn't lost it since, but their direction troubled him. The mountains in these parts were high and sheer, impossible for horses to traverse. The only way, other than climbing over the top, was through a narrow gorge. Single file. Slow, laborious.

"Could be?" echoed Fleming, unable to keep the impatience and frustration out of his voice. "You're the one who should know, Cole!"

"The trail peters out roundabouts here, Captain. They is clever. They know we is hot on their trail and they ain't about to make chasing 'em easy."

"So, what's your bet on this? They have gone through the gorge?"

Cole ran his eyes over the tracks, easy to see in the snow, but only an expert could decipher their meaning. "There are six of 'em, travelling on foot and light because they have let their horses loose. You send your men through that gorge, you is sealing their doom I can tell you that."

"Is that all – *Six*? Are you out of your mind? I have twenty good men here, Cole. We can outrun them within a few hours, I reckon."

"Then you'd be reckoning wrong if you think you'll have twenty men at the end of this, Captain. My advice ...?" He looked Fleming full in the face, unblinking. "You circumnavigate the mountain, cut them off at the far end."

"Circum-*what*?"

"Go around. You give me four of your best men and we'll cut a path over the top, whilst you and the rest make your—"

"Hold on, Cole." Fleming, shielding his eyes against the sun with the flat on one hand across his brow, looked to the top of the mountains, "You'll climb that thing?"

"That's all we have. If you can block the far end of the gorge, we will then come down upon them from above. They'll give it up then, I guarantee it."

"That sure seems like a lot of hard work ... You can do it?"

"I've done it before."

"I bet you have..." Fleming dropped his hand and shook his head. "Going around will take us more than two days. By that time, they will be gone."

"They will not be expecting us to do what I've laid out. They will hole themselves up ready to ambush you."

"Six against twenty? I doubt it."

"They is Apache, Captain. They ain't like other Injuns."

"You said Comanch are the meanest."

"They is, but when it comes to ambush, no one gets anywhere close to Apache. Trust me on this, Captain. Please."

Deep in thought, Fleming chewed away at his bottom lip, looking from the top to the bottom of the mountain range. It seemed to Cole that the cavalry commander was involved in a desperate dispute with himself. The scout prayed he would find the right solution.

After a long pause, the captain blew out a long breath and shook his head. "Nah, we simply ain't got the time, Cole. They will be long gone. I doubt they will ambush us," he quickly held up his hand before Cole could interject once again, "I respect your undoubted knowledge on this Cole, but common sense, if nothing else, tells me they would not try and shoot down an entire cavalry troop. So, we'll go through while you, and your selected men, scale up over the top to cover us."

"Captain, they will kill the officers and NCOs first. The rest of your men will then hightail it out of there quicker than a little 'un who's upturned a wasps' nest."

"Well that's easily fixed." Grinning at his own brainwave, Fleming quickly peeled off his uniform jacket and stuffed it behind the bedroll looped across the rear of his saddle. Sweeping off his hat, he threw it across to a waiting trooper, who grabbed it, wide-eyed with bewilderment. "Toss me your kepi, trooper." Recovering, the young cavalryman took off his headgear and, not wishing to offend, gently eased his horse over to his commanding officer. Fleming took the kepi, positioned it at an appropriately jaunty angle and, looking smug, nodded towards Cole. "There! I'm now just an ordinary trooper, or at least I'll look that way to any pesky Apache. Don't you think so, Cole?"

Exasperated, Cole decided it was best to look away. Clearly, Captain Fleming was not going to be persuaded of the foolishness of his plan. "I'll start my men up the rock face immediately," said Cole and signalled to the nearby sergeant, who knew exactly what to do. Within a few minutes, Cole had his men assembled in front of him, carbines and water-bottles at the ready. Cole dismounted. "Give us a head start, Cap'n, before you go through."

"I will that, Cole. See you at the other end."

Grunting, Cole motioned for the gathered troopers to begin their steady and careful ascent.

They were only five minutes into the climb when they heard the first gunshot.

In accompaniment to mounting gunfire, Cole urged his men ever upwards. The climb proved arduous; the cold biting deep. Even so, by the time they made the crest all of them were soaked in sweat. Worming his way to the edge of the rise, Cole squinted down into the gorge. Fleming and his men were there, scurrying behind cover like so many ants. One lay spread-eagled on the ground, clearly dead. Reaching for the eyeglasses at his hip, Cole adjusted the focus ring to get a more detailed view of what was happening down there amongst the hard, unforgiving rocks. As he scanned the area, he could see his prophesy from earlier had come true – the one fallen dead was the poor trooper who had donned Fleming's cap and tunic.

"Ah, darn it," breathed another young trooper slithering up beside him, taking the proffered field glasses and instantly ducking his head down in reaction to a distant gunshot. He put the glasses to his eyes and hissed. "This is bad, Mr Cole."

"Seems that way." The scout rolled over onto his back and signalled for the others to keep low. "We have to try and get into a position where we have the advantage."

The young trooper handed back the glasses. "They look as though they got round the back of the captain. There's two of 'em pinning our boys down, picking them off every time they show themselves."

Scanning the area again, Cole grunted. "There's one is at the front, blocking off any chance of moving forward. They're hemmed in."

"And the others?" asked another trooper from a position some feet away from the edge and well out of sight.

"I can't see 'em," said Cole. Then, he cursed loudly. "The horses! They've circled back to take the horses." He pounded the ground with his fist. "Darn it! They mean to take the cavalry horses and leave Fleming and his men with no means to travel save on foot."

"I'll stop him," said the young trooper quickly. Already he was beginning his descent when Cole grabbed his arm. They exchanged a look. Cole recognised him of course but, as always, he could not remember the youth's name. He'd done well when they had first hunted down this group of Apaches, learning fast. Cole also remembered his easy manner, his intelligence and quick-thinking. If he could choose any of these men to watch his back, it would be this young trooper. He went to speak, but the youth got in there first. "There's no choice, Mr Cole. You know it."

"Yes, I suppose I do." He gave a wry smile and squeezed the trooper's arm harder still. "You take care down there, son. You'll not hear any of 'em when they comes up behind you."

"You know I've held my own against these savages before, Mr Cole. I know what to do."

Acquiescing, Cole nodded and watched the young man scramble back down the way he had come only moments before. He said, to no one in particular, "What's his name again?"

"Vance. Hyrum Vance," said another, then added in a low, heavy sounding voice, "He's eighteen years old."

Cole winced and looked again through his glasses, saying through gritted teeth, "If he saves those horses, I'll request a citation to U.S. Army headquarters in Denver for his bravery."

"No one in our troop has ever had one of those, Mr Cole."

"Well, it's past time that you did. Anyone who comes out here to face Apache has more sand than can be found in Death Valley."

"We don't have no say in any of that. We just follow orders is all."

Straining his neck, Cole stared at the trooper. "And what's your name, son?"

"Crevis. Boys back in the barracks call me Buster. This here is Larry McDonald and Jason Spooney." The other two nodded without uttering a word.

"We all have choices," said Cole, "and the choices start at the top. If governors and senators and the like hadn't been in the pockets of railroad tycoons, we never would have had so much trouble with the natives."

"But they is savages," snapped McDonald. "Whatever their excuses, we can't allow them to do what they do, murdering and burning and the like. No sir, we cannot allow such things."

"McDonald is it?" The trooper nodded. "Son, I reckon we is all savages at heart. What we have done to these people is nothing more than rape and pillage. They is only giving back what we first gave them. I believe that is something your ancestors were well accustomed to when the English ripped out your homeland during the Highland Clearances."

McDonald gaped at the scout. "I'm impressed with your knowledge, sir."

"I'm a scholar of such things and I see the pattern being repeated everywhere I look."

"I bow to your learning, nevertheless, these Apache are unlike anyone else."

"Perhaps in their efficiency, but not their methods." Cole returned to the view below. "As far as I can tell, they have no awareness of us, so we have to get down there and help Vance to take them out. You'll need to move slow and careful, keep your wits about and do not discharge your firearms until I give the signal."

"And if you fall, Mr Cole?"

Cole chuckled, "Then it's every man for himself, but I won't be caring too much about any of that."

"I'm scared," said Spooney, his voice trembling.

"We all is, son," said Cole. He smiled reassuringly. "Just keep your head down and do as I do. All will be fine."

No one spoke. Cole returned the field glasses to their leather case and motioned the men forward. As one, they wormed their way over the crest and began their descent into the gorge.

CHAPTER NINE

Hyrum Vance

Scrambling over the many rocks and boulders, often losing his footing, which caused him to jar his knees painfully, Vance stopped beside a particularly large boulder and slumped down behind it. Tearing off his kepi, he wiped the sweat from his brow with the back of his hand. This was not what he'd joined the army for. They said it was good pay with three square a day, adventurous, riding out across the plain, but with no danger. He never paused to fathom why they were recruiting so fervently, and he put his name at the foot of the paper, lying about his age without a thought. Back home, his sickly mother broke down at the news, clawing at his shirt front, shaking him, begging him not to go. His younger brother, Nathanial, looked on with a gleam in his eye, chest swelled up with pride. "He's gonna ride with the U.S. Cavalry, Ma! Don't take on so." She rounded on her second son and gave him such a slap across the face that the thirteen-year-old fell to his knees and burst into tears, more from shock and indignation than anything else.

Seizing her by the arm, Vance turned her to him, his eyes also full of tears. "Oh Ma, why must you take on so – why must you make me feel so guilty!"

"Guilty? *I'm afraid!*"

Gaping at her, his grip loosened, and she tore herself free. "There's no need to be. There'll be no fighting and I can send money home every month. It's for the best, Ma, it truly is."

She pulled out a square of linen from her sleeve and used it to dab away at her wet face. "No fighting? Old Santiago over at the livery said there are stories coming down from South Dakota that they've discovered gold up there and some of the Indians are making threats. There's talk of war, Hyrum!"

"War? It's not going to come to war, Ma, whatever it is that is happening up there." Towering over her, he rested his hands on her shoulders. From this close, he could see how weary and old she looked. "South Dakota? That is hundreds of miles away. Besides, all those Indians, they will be in reservations soon. The recruiting sergeant told me that there are only the occasional stragglers who break out and cause mischief. It's all perfectly safe."

A bullet slapped against a nearby rock, ricocheting away at a wild angle and Vance, coming out of his reverie with a jolt, flung himself face down into the dirt. Sucking in air, his head pounding with fear, he clung onto his carbine and wondered what to do. His movement towards the boulder had been slow and cautious. He felt sure nobody could have spotted him.

But, of course, these were Apache.

He waited, forcing himself to count slowly to thirty. Somewhere beyond the cover of the large rock, more shots rang out, returning fire from his comrades no doubt. Tensing himself, he rolled over and got to his knees, chancing a quick look over the rim of the boulder.

He spotted the Apache warrior almost immediately. He wore a bright red shirt and black bandana, the flesh of his naked legs burned the colour of leather. Dipping back out of sight, Vance counted again. If he was quick enough, he could shoot the Indian, break cover and find the others. His orders were to gather the horses, but the thought of felling a savage was too great.

He felt rather than heard something behind him. He span around and for a moment caught the flash of bright eyes, a grimace fixed on a chewed-up face burnished by the sun. He groaned as the knife went in deep. The Apache's face was so close, and he was smiling. For a moment, terror seized Vance's body, but he somehow managed to summon the strength to grip his attacker's arm. He held on, gazing into the other's eyes, hypnotised by their intensity, and all he could think about was a warm, swirling sensation, dragging him forever downwards. "Oh, dear Lord," he moaned, the carbine slipping from fingers growing numb. The Apache titled his head, the smile broadening and he slipped a free hand around Vance's neck, cupping his head to gain more leverage as he pushed the knife deeper still.

"Go to your ancestors," said the Apache in a low, soothing voice and he pushed again.

Vance held onto the man's arm, awestruck by his strength, seduced by the curious feelings washing over him, feelings of calmness, surrender. He knew the blood was pumping out of him, in a thick, warm torrent. He thought he should cry out, try and warn the others, but the Apache's reassuring smile made him realise that nothing could save any of them now and the fight left him. The Apache gently lowered him to the ground, the knife still deep, then slowly withdrew it. Vance gazed into the face of his conqueror, thought he saw something else, regret perhaps, and then there was nothing.

CHAPTER TEN

Cole

Gunfire increased the deeper into the gorge Cole and his men went. More of it seemed to be coming from the far end, drawing fire from the troopers. Fleming was waving his hand like someone possessed, his teeth flashing white in a face red with rage. "Cole, the horses!"

Keeping low and close to the side of the gorge down which they had ascended, Cole and his men scurried along, finding whatever cover they could, edging their way ever closer to where they had tethered the horses.

Crevis spotted him first, drawing up to a sudden stop, Cole and the others almost crashing into him. Then Cole saw it too and he lowered his head and silently cursed.

Hyrum Vance lay pressed against a rock, eyes wide open, staring into nothing, his torso soaked through with blood. Beyond him, where the Apaches had once been, there was now nothing but open plain. Another soldier lay face down in the dirt, dead. The horses gone.

"What do we do now?" wailed Spooney, falling to his knees. "Those horses had our canteens and everything. We're gonna die out here!"

"Shut up," snapped McDonald, rounding on his fellow-soldier, taking him by the arms and shaking him as if he were a naughty child.

"You quit that, Jason. None of us is gonna die out here, ain't that right, Cole?"

Cole met the young Scot's desperate stare and did his best to sound positive. "I reckon. But we'll need water if we're gonna make it back to the fort. We're two days out, and that's by horseback."

"Oh, dear Lord," said Crevis, crumbling to the ground. "You can multiply that by ten if we're travelling on foot."

"*Ten days?*" yelled Spooney. "Are you out of your mind? How can we walk ten days without water?"

"There's the snow," said McDonald quickly, becoming animated with his idea. "What do you think, Mr Cole? We can survive by drinking the snow."

"Yes," said Cole slowly, "we can, although snow don't give you that much. Enough maybe, to keep us alive. But the nights will be cold, boys. Maybe too cold. It was different when we had the tents. Outside," he looked at the sky, at its uniform blue, "in this, with no cloud cover, we might freeze."

"Jeez, you're just full of laughs, ain't you Cole." Crevis stood up to his full height, confident he was out of range of the remaining Apache at the far end of the gorge. "I say we rush that lone savage, kill him and take whatever he has, then we can—"

"I got a better idea," said Cole, staring down the gorge. "But it's something I need to do on my own."

CHAPTER ELEVEN

Julia

Sometime before his confrontation with the Apaches, Cole had ridden into the town of Feathernest on a very different kind of mission. She had not been so hard to find. Perhaps she meant it that way. Slowing down to a walk, he spotted her straight away sat in a rocking chair looking like a million dollars and he noted how her eyes followed him. He wondered what he should do now. She'd gunned down an escaped criminal after aiding him in his escape, clubbed Sterling to the ground but then balanced the scales when she later saved Cole's life. Seeing her again, bold as could be, stirred him up inside. Already he was formulating reasons for not bringing her in to face justice. He knew he'd have to find a way because watching her dangle from the end of a rope was not something he ever wished to contemplate. So, mind swirling with confusion over finding a solution, he guided his horse to the livery stable.

From where she sat, Julia could not help but smile. He looked as good as he ever did in that saddle, his back straight, his face tanned and hard looking, just the way she remembered. Old Mrs Roman, who had taken her in the day she first rolled up, poured out a glass of lemonade, cleared her throat and fixed Julia a look akin to that of a schoolteacher. "Is that him?"

Julia did her best to suppress a young-girl-like giggle but failed. Feeling the heat move across her jawline and rise to her cheeks, she turned and brushed away a lock of golden hair from her face. "Yes. That's Reuben."

"He looks a fine man," Mrs Roman said, sipping at her drink. Julia regarded her with a keen interest. The older woman smiled. "I remember the day I first laid eyes on my Clancy. Felt my heart swell right up into my throat, I did." Unconsciously, a hand fell to her breast as her eyes grew misty with the memory. "I couldn't speak. Is that how it is with you?"

"Well," she gave another short laugh, "perhaps not quite the same, but yes, I must admit the sight of him so lean and strong ..." She shook her head. "There's a strength within him I have not known in any other man I've met. I feel safe with him."

"And yet you chose to ride away."

"I wasn't sure how he'd react after what happened. I'd spent a lot of my time making plans on how to deal with Burroughs, plotting my revenge. I wasn't sure if Reuben would accept what I did. He's a man of honour."

"Accept what? The Killing of that horrible man, you mean?"

Julia's eyes bulged wide. "How—?"

Mrs Roman gave a tiny shrug and returned her empty glass to the small table beside her. "You were crying out in your sleep first night you stayed here. Rolling around and lashing out like you was in a fight or something. Then, when you shouted, 'Rot in hell' and a few other, much more choice words, I surmised something quite awful had happened."

"Oh my, Mrs Roman, why didn't you *say* something?"

"To be honest, I didn't know what to think." She looked again at the tall stranger, whom Julia had referred to as Reuben, dressed in buckskin and black, calf-length boots, leading his horse to the livery. "The only thing I do not like is that gun of his, the way it is holstered at a slant across his middle. Clancy often told me of gunmen he'd seen who wore their guns like that."

"He's not a gunman," said Julia quickly, "he's a U.S. Army scout."

"So that's how he found you? He tracked you down?"

Julia's grin widened again, showing her even, white teeth. "No. I think it was more likely the telegram I sent him." She leaned over and squeezed Mrs Roman's hand. "I did a lot of thinking, most of it about how he helped me. I decided I wanted security, a period of calm. I believe he could give me that, so I messaged him."

"So, you no longer wish to run away from the killing?"

Another squeeze before Julia returned to her embroidery. "I'll not try and wrap that up into something it is not. I ended that despicable man's life for what he did. I'm not proud of it, but I don't regret it."

"Despite it being a mortal sin?"

Julia sighed, laid down her needle, and was about to say something when she noticed Reuben Cole emerging from the livery stable. She saw him taking off his battered hat and slapping it against his thigh, a tiny cloud of dust springing up. As he replaced it, he caught her eye and smiled.

Without averting her eyes, she continued talking to Mrs Roman. "I understand your point of view, I do. And yes, I could have watched Burroughs swing for what he did, but ..." She shook her head. "I was consumed ... *consumed* by my hatred for him. I planned it, down to the very last moment. I hooked him and drew him in so that his trust of me was total. I wanted him to realise, as he breathed his last, the depth of my betrayal and the enormity of his error."

"In other words, you wanted him to suffer."

"Indeed, I did. But it's not in my nature. I had to steel myself to see it through right to the very end. I am not a murderess, I wanted revenge. Against him, and nobody else. I'm hoping Reuben will see it my way."

"And if he doesn't?"

"Then I'll face the consequences." Her eyes stared hard at the other woman. "I'm ready, Mrs Roman, don't get me wrong. I did a bad thing and if I have to face trial, then so be it." She straightened her back as Cole approached.

She noticed his smile never faltered.

"Mistress Julia," said Cole, doffing his hat. He looked at Mrs Roman and did the same, "Ma'am."

"Good day, Mr Cole," said Mrs Roman. "Julia has been telling me something about you. An Army scout so I understand."

"Indeed, I am, Ma'am."

"And have scouted your way here, to take Julia back."

"That," said Cole with meaning, "is up to her."

Laying down her embroidery, Julia brushed away some imaginary specs of dust from her dress. "I'm willing," she said.

Sighing, Cole put his hands on his hips and smiled. "Then perhaps I could trouble you for a glass of that delicious looking lemonade. It sure is hot out here today."

Returning his smile, Julia went to lift the jug, but Mrs Roman was already there, chuckling to herself. "Seems like justice has been served after all, Julia."

"Indeed so," said Julia, watching Mrs Roman filling up the glass, licking her lips as the sharp tang of fresh lemons hit the back of her throat. She passed the glass across to Cole.

"What's done is done," said Cole, taking the glass and draining it in one. He smacked his lips and stared at the empty glass with satisfaction. "We can't turn back the clock and no point in trying."

"And your report will declare such a thing?"

Cole frowned at Mrs Roman. "Report? What report?" He winked a little impishly. "This isn't an official visit, Ma'am." He smiled and looked at Julia for a long time. "Purely social."

Both women laughed, and Cole held out his hand for another glass of lemonade.

CHAPTER TWELVE

Hold-Up

The spread's small size meant it proved manageable and with Cole away so often this fact was a godsend. Yes, Julia would have preferred more space for their horses and the two barns required urgent fixing, but all in all nothing would be too daunting over the coming months. Even as the winter took hold, the snow from the mountain tops encroaching downwards to nibble at the outer edges of the fields, she felt comfortable and safe.

Sometimes, if he was not on duty, Sterling Roose would ride over from town and keep her company. She liked Sterling and, now that he had completely forgiven her for laying him out cold when she helped Burroughs to escape, they were good friends, sharing stories and laughter over freshly made coffee. She'd feel a tug at her heart when Cole's friend would announce his departure and she'd stand on the porch watching him disappearing into the distance.

She had previously known long periods of solitude when, married to her late husband, business would keep him away, sometimes for weeks at a time. Of course, back then, she did not know what that 'business' was, and she spent her time in quiet pursuits such as reading, embroidery and taking long walks around their vast ranch. So unlike now when, sleeves rolled up, she'd wash and scrub, fix and mend, no two days ever being the same. Sometimes she missed her former life, the peace, the opportunities to contemplate, study the wisdom of ages past through the many books in the library, but most of the time she relished her new life. Except for one thing. The anxiety.

Often, Cole would ride into the ranch late in the mornings to announce orders had been delivered, orders which meant he would have to leave again. In any given month, he would be out scouting at least every other week. Usually it was mundane tracking duties. Sometimes horses broken free from army stables, fences rotten and easily knocked through, sometimes hunting down deserters, of which there were many. But sometimes it was raiders, be they disaffected ex-army or, more worryingly, Indians. She always knew when it was the latter as Cole could never keep anything from his face. The deep lines of concern written in the creases around his eyes spoke volumes and she'd feel the tendrils of fear creeping across her back once again.

It was during one of his many absences that Julia took the flat wagon into town to pick up supplies. She tended to make the journey every three months or so. Although it was not an arduous journey, it was long and, especially with the cold biting so deep, she wished there was some other way to stock up with oats, barley, coffee, beans, and rice. But there wasn't. Unlike her previous life with her husband, there were no servants to help. Cole had made this abundantly clear when he first invited her to his home. "My father has a place," he told her. "It's large, the house well-built and decorated to a high standard, but I'm not my father. We went our separate ways and I chose the army life. It means I'm a man of meagre means. My home is simple, but comfortable, I guess. I rear horses and manage to sell one or two, but there are no other means and I haven't much to offer a woman such as you. I'm not telling you this to dissuade you, Julia, merely to lay everything before you, openly and honestly."

She had smiled at him, knowing the circumstances were not perfect by any means, but they were all she had. For now. Stroking his rough cheek, she said to him, "Reuben, I'm not looking for a knight in shining armour, just someone who will treat me right and who will never lie."

Blushing, he looked away. "Well, I guess that could be me."

He did take her to his father's place. Not to visit, merely to stand on the hill overlooking the spread, gazing at the house with the smoke trailing from the double chimneys, knowing it was occupied.

"Do you never visit him?"

Cole shrugged. "Sometimes. He has his own life and he's made it plain, on more than one occasion, he does not approve of my choices. He made a fortune importing exotic spices and tea from the east. A sailor, he'd risen as mate on one of the great clippers that set out from San Francisco. He made contacts, developed a network and ..." He gave a short laugh and waved his hand over the vistas before them, "This is the result."

"It's very impressive, Reuben. It's a wonder you didn't follow him in his trade."

"I have no interest in it. My life has always been the prairie. Perhaps, when he's gone, I'll move in ... Who knows."

Now, moving down the main track of the small town, she pushed the memories aside as she steered the wagon towards the large merchandise store. Bringing the pony to a halt, she drew back the hand brake. Turning, she gathered her cloth bag containing her money. The street was quiet, the snow well settled on the ground and those people who did shuffle by were huddled deep inside thick coats, scarves, and hats. Heads down, nobody acknowledged her, not that such a thing concerned her too much. Everyone had their own business to attend to, never mind hers.

Stepping down from the wagon, she was about to mount the steps to the store door when the unmistakeable sound of a pistol being cocked brought her to a sudden halt.

A figure, swathed in voluminous black coat, gloves, scarf and hat, emerged out of nowhere. He gestured with the gun in his hand and spoke, voice muffled behind the scarf concealing the bottom part of his face, a face ruby red with cold. "I'll take the bag, miss."

Unable to register much of what was happening, Julia collapsed on the buckboard steps, rigid with fear, all her attention focused on the huge, black pistol aimed directly towards her.

"Give me the bag NOW!"

She jumped, somehow finding the strength to move. She glanced

45

around, hoping someone, anyone would come to her aid, but mere phantoms glided by swathed against the cold. It was as if she were alone in a world suddenly turned brutal and uncaring.

"Don't even think about crying out, or I'll shoot you dead."

She looked at him, the menace clear in his grey eyes and she knew he spoke truth. Swallowing down hard, she managed to say, "I have only about twenty bucks."

"That's more than enough for me." He thrust out his hand. "Pass it over."

With little choice, Julia reached for the bag, turning away from her assailant for a brief moment. But in that small flicker of time, it happened.

Yelping, she turned to see another, much younger man in tweed jacket and cord trousers, grappling with the would-be robber, punching him, gripping his gun hand, slamming him to the ground. She watched, hands clamped to her mouth, as the two men wrestled in the snow, rolling over, kicking, punching, and clawing. The young one had his hand wrapped around the other's wrist, twisting the gun away, out of danger, whilst he repeatedly jabbed his other fist into the robber's ribs.

A knee came up, the robber squealed, releasing the hold on his gun and the young man stood up, triumphant, breathing hard, the Colt in his hand now.

"Get up," snarled the younger man. The robber, groaning, got to his feet with some difficulty. He looked up, the scarf having fallen down to reveal a bewildered expression on what was otherwise a handsome, almost angelic face. Without a pause, the younger man landed a full, swinging punch to the other's jaw and dumped him to the ground where he lay, motionless.

The young man turned to her. "Are you all right, ma'am?"

She gazed in disbelief. This close, Julia recognised him at once, so there could be no escaping who he was.

"Oh my ..." was all she could manage to say.

CHAPTER THIRTEEN

Nolan's Journal

I'd struck up something of a friendship with a thin looking fella by the name of Sam Caine. He was pleasant enough, with a mop of blond hair set upon his smooth face which lent him something of a boyish air. I could understand why the ladies seemed drawn to him so much. He'd laugh about that sometimes, winking, "Oh, there's something else too, but you'll have to guess what." He worked hard out on the range and it became something of a ritual for us to ride out to the far-off edges of the spread to spend the morning repairing the fences. Alone, with just the sky and the distant mountains for company, we'd talk about all sorts of things. It was during one such time, as we sat with our backs against a rocky outcrop munching down the corn bread dear old Miss Tomkins from the kitchen made us – I think she had something of a thing for Sam – that he told me why he was there.

"I'd got into bad company," he said, staring into space as if the memories were difficult to recall, "and took to drinking way too much. I went into town one evening. I was working for Chisum on one of his ranches back then. Anyways, we got to gambling and drinking and a fight broke out, as they usually did." Sam picked at a tuft of grass and put it between his teeth. He shook his head, growing angry. "One of our bunch, a man called Entwistle, he gunned down another who was playing and that was that. We skedaddled but the town got up a posse and ..." He pulled out the grass and threw it away in disgust. "I been running ever since."

"But you didn't kill him."

"No, but I was there, and I was drunk. To be honest, I couldn't swear what I did or didn't do. All I remember is when I woke up next morning we was out on the range and the first thing I did was to check my gun. It had six bullets in the cylinder, so ..."

We continued working after our little talk and from that point we were close. Often on a Saturday night we'd go into town and have ourselves a good time, but none of it to excess. Shapiro did not want me to draw attention to myself. But talk of Sam being involved in a shooting, whether deliberately or not, got me to thinking I could use his undoubted experience in a rough and tumble to help me out with Julia.

So, I came up with the idea of holding her up and me, the hero of the hour, coming to her rescue. If Sam wondered what it was all leading to, he never asked. I gave him a hundred dollars to help and that seemed to satisfy him more than anything.

I'd been going over to Cole's ranch too, whenever I found the right moment. Naturally, I had to be careful unless someone saw me and got to asking questions. But, as far as I knew at the time, nobody did see me. I'd lie down on the rise which overlooked the little spread and I'd watch her for most of the day. I would see her coming out to look after the horses or work in the vegetable patch. Occasionally a wiry individual who I knew as Sterling Roose would visit and they'd stay indoors for a long time. I wondered about that. Something told me that the life Julia was leading was not the one she wanted. Cole, so she confided in me, was almost always out on the range, fulfilling his duties with the Army. Her loneliness ate away at her.

It was while returning to the ranch after one of these visits that I was called over by a big cowpuncher by the name of Lawrenson. He was grinning, showing a full set of chipped, blackened teeth as he stood outside the bunkhouse. As I dismounted, he could hardly contain his eagerness to grab me by the arm and march me inside. No one else was around. It was when he closed the door and locked it that I knew something bad was going to happen.

"All righty," he said securing the door, his back to me. "I need you to tell me where it is you go every afternoon." Before I could offer a response, he swung around in a sudden blur and landed a swinging right across my jaw that put me flat on my backside.

With my head swimming I had no time to react as those big, beefy hands were hauling me to my feet.

"Where d'you go?"

His knee came up and slammed straight into my groin. The pain exploded right across my lower body and I thought for one horrible moment I was going to vomit. This was my only thought, my mind in a mess, and I sagged in his strong hands and blubbered. He struck me flat-handed across the face and followed through with another solid punch. My legs went from under me and I hit the floor so hard I heard my teeth rattle.

I don't know for how long I lay there. The pain was blinding, and my face felt like it had been put through as meat grinder. Weird shapes and colours danced in front my eyes but other than that, I couldn't make out anything as I blinked and struggled to focus. As if that wasn't bad enough, as I tried to push myself upright, a huge deluge of fiercely cold water hit my face, stinging me into full consciousness. Spluttering, confused, but alert, I rolled over and sat up.

Big old Lawrenson leant against the far wall, arms folded across his barrel chest, grinning like he'd won the biggest prize of all. "So, I been watching you, boy, and I want to know where you're going. I also want to know why you've got so friendly with that Caine boy. Seems to me *unusual* and I'm thinking you and him have found a nice little place of your own that you can hunker up together real close."

"What?" I blinked, wiped my mouth, and even managed a tiny, scoffing laugh. "Are you out of your mind?"

"No shame in it, boy." He leered. "Happens all the time out here."

"Shame in *what?*" He gave me an exaggerated wink and I felt my stomach heave as I realised the meaning. "No, no, not to me it don't happen. You got it wrong, Lawrenson. *Very* wrong."

"Is that right?"

"Yes, it is." I went to stand up but before I could even get myself half-raised, he was on me again, taking me by the throat and running me across the room like I was a little child in his enormous grip. He smashed me against the far wall, knocking what air was left in my lungs straight out into his face. I wailed, "Please Lawrenson, don't hit me no more."

Laughing now, he put his big, greasy face straight up against me. "Tell me the truth, little boy. Tell me the truth or I'll not stopping hitting you so bad even your own mommy won't recognise me."

"Oh God."

His grip tightened. I grabbed at his massive forearm, but it was useless, his strength was too much. He was going to kill me, that I knew for sure.

His mouth pressed against my ear, "We is a God-fearing community in this ranch. Mr Rancine, he is a forgiving man, but he lives his life by the Good Book and degenerates are not welcome here. I went to him with my concerns and he told me to find out the truth." He pressed himself even closer. "The truth."

"Please, it's not true what you think."

The pressure from his fingers eased a little, allowing me to speak more easily. "You want me to think you and him have not had any ... relations?"

"I ..." I swallowed. I knew there was only one way to get out this alive, one way to give myself an edge. So, I lied. I took a deep breath and said, as feebly as possible, "All right. It's true—"

"I knew it."

But if I was expecting an eruption of anger, I was wrong. Instead, he released his hold around my throat, stepped back half a pace, a curious softness appearing around his eyes. "You and him, you is lovers?"

I nodded, averting my eyes from his. "I'm sorry. I know it's wrong, but out here, like you say, it's difficult, difficult to keep to a natural path."

"Hot dang." He licked his lips, the sight almost causing me to vomit, this time for real. "I just knew it was true. I just knew it."

"Will you tell Mr Rancine? I need this job, Lawrenson, I truly do."

"I won't tell him, no."

"Thank you."

"But only if you do something for me." He leaned closer again, his lips slack, that great tongue lolling out. "I want you to get close to me, the way you do with Caine."

It all happened so quickly then. Even with the burning continuing to spread across my loins, with my head all full of cotton wool, this horrible, disgusting man with his loathsome mind, it all just snapped. My knife was in my hands before I knew what was happening and I thrust it in him with all my strength. Gasping, he looked down at the blade in horror. Taking my chance, I stabbed him again, not once, but several times until he collapsed onto the floor, writhing in agony and disbelief. Blood frothed and gurgled out of his disgusting mouth. I stood and watched him, my hand and arm covered in him and I looked into his fat face and wanted to laugh.

And then he died.

Some moments later, I am not sure how many, I stumbled out into the fresh air. Steadying myself against the bunkhouse exterior wall, I did what I could to settle myself. Yes, I have killed before, but to be that close, to smell him, to witness the life dying in his eyes, nothing could prepare me for the horror of that.

I made sure nobody saw me as I stepped up to Sam Caine. He was in the little workshop next to the livery, fixing up saddles, stirrups, and stuff. He gave me a quick smile as I slouched in beside him.

"You look like you been working hard," he said. "That's a lot of blood. What you been doing, calving?"

"Yes, I have," I lied. "Can I ask you; do you know Lawrenson?"

"Ugh," he gave a little shiver which I hoped meant he was filled with as much disgust at the thought of that lump of lard as I was. I was proved right. "I hate him, always leering at me. I think he's not a ladies' man, if you get my meaning."

"I do. And can I add, just as a little hors d'oeuvre ..." He gave me a puzzled look. "It's French."

"You can speak French?" he shook his head in wonder and returned to unpicking the stitching around the pommel of the saddle he was working on.

"I can speak lots of things. My momma was Creole."

"You're kidding me."

"Oui."

He sniggered. "You're crazy, you know that. So, Lawrenson. What's he done?"

"Nothing. It's what I've done to him."

So, I told him and as I spoke, Caine grew paler and paler until I thought he was going to pass out. I helped him put away his tools, which gave him something to do and hopefully calm him down a little. Together, we then returned to the bunkhouse. I'd already rolled the big cow-punch in a taupe and now we took to working hard and fast. We carried him out to where we left the horses and tied him up across the back of mine. Lawrenson was big and heavy, and it took us a lot of effort but at last we had him secured. We scanned every angle, but nobody was around. The sun, high in the sky, beat down strong, despite winter being here. Most of the cowboys would be out with the herd, so we pretty much had the time to ourselves. At last, when the grizzly work was done, we rode out across the ranch to beyond the far fences. We put Lawrenson in a dried-up riverbed about four or so miles from the main ranch, covering him with big rocks and brush. Nobody would find him unless they were looking.

We stood there, hands on hips, breathing hard. An exchange of looks, but no words. I guessed that was more than Lawrenson deserved.

Later, we sat down at the trestles outside the bunkhouse and did our best to swallow our supper. Nobody spoke to us. Around about fifteen of us were there, heads down, the cook, a Mexican named Felipe, spooning out dollops of gristle and gravy. It looked vile and tasted worse.

"What you gonna do now?" whispered Caine. I checked no one else was close, leaned towards him and I laid out my plan, nice, slow, and quiet. He had to pretend to hold up Julia and I would punch him, not hard. I promised him that. His expression said he didn't believe me. "Maybe you're gonna take the opportunity to dole out all your hatred and anger onto me. Kick me from here to Kingdom Come."

"Don't be silly." I gave him a wink. "You're my only friend."

"Let's hope."

I didn't comment, deciding to return to my meal. It was to be me my last at the ranch because next day we would get ready to meet Julia. I'd been watching her and knew her routine. Tomorrow was her weekly stopover at the merchandise store over in town. It was all worked out and nothing could go wrong. Nothing.

It was when we were preparing for bed that the unlooked-for trouble occurred. The door to the bunkhouse crashed open and in strode Mr Rancine breathing hard, flanked by two of his top trail bosses. All looked mean, clad in long dusters, guns tied down, hats making 'em seem larger than they actually were, which was all part of the act, I guess.

"You boys seen Lawrenson?"

They were six of us in that bunkhouse, including me and Caine, every one of us in varying stages of undress and, as Rancine's eyes roamed over us, his expression turned to one of disgust.

"Speak up," he spat, making the most it by letting his right hand rest on the butt of his ivory handled Colt.

"Ain't seen him since this morning," said a hasty little squirt by the name of Harrowby.

"Nor me," said the others in quick succession.

"Why, Mr Rancine," said Caine and I almost gagged as I tried my utmost not the glare at him, "what's happened?"

"He's gone missing," said Perryman, one of the trail bosses. "You sure you ain't seen him?" He levelled his eyes on me. "Word is you and him were kinda friendly."

"I would not say that, Mr Perryman."

"Then what would you say, boy?" Rancine's eyes narrowed dangerously, and I felt myself drowning under his harsh gaze.

"I'm not his friend," I managed to say.

"Others have seen you and him talking, sometimes real intimate like."

"No sir. Not in any friendly way. Mr Lawrenson never did like me, sir. Always making me do extra duties and things, never allowing me near the steers. He often laughed at me, the way I rode, said I needed lessons."

"So, where is he?"

"Mr Rancine, sir, I honestly do not know. Last I saw him, like Harrowby said, was this morning."

"You sure?"

"I swear it, sir."

"Because others have said they saw him heading this way around noon time. Where were you at noon time?"

"I was over on the far end, sir, like I always am, mending fences, replacing posts."

"Anyone vouch for you?"

"I can, Mr Rancine," said Caine. "We came back around supper time, having worked out there most of the day."

They all stood looking, chewing at their lips, or twitching their fingers around their guns. They seemed to be measuring up everything we'd said, and it took them a long time.

"All right," said Rancine at last and, shooting us a final disgusted look, flounced out with the trail bosses close behind.

We sat there in the semi-darkness, the only light from a small oil-lamp in the corner casting a feeble, sickly light making everything seem creepy and a little unreal.

"We all know he had desires," said Harrowby from his bed. "Unnatural they were."

"I wouldn't know," I said.

"Could be a reason."

"Reason for what?"

"Why he's gone missing."

"I don't get you."

"Oh, you know … Perhaps he figured you knew how he was, and he decided to cut loose before Mr Rancine confronted him. Mr Rancine, he's all into that old Biblical way of punishments. I reckon if there was real proof about Lawrenson, Mr Rancine would string him up. What do you say to that?"

"I'd say you could be right – but I'd also say I had nothing to do with it. He never spoke to me about such things. Maybe to you, Harrowby as you seem to know an awful lot about it."

He was half off the bed. Even in the semi-darkness I could see him coming at me, fists bunched, "Why you ..."

But I was there first, and punched him hard in the jaw, knocking back onto his bed. He hit the edge with the small of his back and jack-knifed sideways to the floor, squealing. One of the others went to stand up and Caine stopped them dead as he drew his gun. "Just give it up boys," he said in that calm, unsettling way of his. They all did as he bid and when Harrowby struggled to his knees I put a left across his face and that was that.

From that point on we both knew we could no longer stay there, no matter what.

CHAPTER FOURTEEN

Julia

He helped her into a chair in the little teashop on the corner. She was shaking and he ordered tea.

"Is she all right?" asked the wizened waitress, a white-haired lady of indeterminate age, who fluttered anxiously around them.

"She will be," he said and leaned across to look at her.

Julia brought her eyes up and a fleeting smile crossed her face. Outside, the would-be assailant had already made himself scarce. "We should inform the sheriff," she said in a tired, frightened voice.

"I think I recognised him."

She raised her eyebrows. "Oh? Who is he?"

"One of the cowboys from the Rancine spread. Name of Harrowby."

"Then at least we can get the sheriff to ride on out there, confront him."

"Yeah, we could, but I've left there now. I was working for 'em, and I needed the job, but their methods, well, they ain't that comfortable for a young, ignorant boy like me." He grinned.

"You're not so ignorant, Trooper."

He leaned back, the grin still evident. "So, you remember me, Miss Julia?"

"I sure do." She paused as the tea arrived. The cup rattled against the saucer as the old lady's trembling hand settled it down on the table. Julia smiled. "Thank you." She took a sip before settling her gaze upon the man opposite. "You were there when they arrested Sergeant Burroughs and again later when he escaped."

"My recollection is that it was you who helped him escape."

"Well, I suppose we both have our reasons for why we ran away." She took another drink, replaced the cup, and studied it for some time. "And now you've come back."

"Just in the nick of time!"

"Yes. So it would seem. Does Reuben Cole know you've come back?"

His eyes flickered, betraying something. Fear, nervousness? She couldn't say, but there was something making him feel uncomfortable.

"You needn't worry," she continued, "Cole has much bigger fish to catch. Right now, he's out searching for some escaped Apache."

"Dangerous work."

"Indeed, it is, Mr Nolan."

He sucked in his breath and sat back, arms crossing over his chest. "I don't go by that name no more. It's another part of me I'd rather leave behind."

"Like I say, I wouldn't worry about Cole."

"I'm not. To be honest, it's that other scout I laid out cold who causes me most concern. Roose?"

"Sterling? Sterling is a good man, honest, straight. He is looking to be sheriff of this town, so perhaps he might be someone you need to steer clear of." Finishing her tea with a loud smacking of lips, she studied him, searching for further reaction. "All of what happened back then is pretty much done and dusted, Mr Nolan. We both made mistakes, things we regret. We no longer have to mention it."

"The past you mean?"

She nodded. "I am in your debt for what you did today, so if there is anything I can do in return ..."

She left it there, the invitation, waiting for him to spring. He took his time then slowly, his arms unfolded, shoulders relaxing, and his own smile developed. "To be honest, there is something ..."

"I thought as much."

Slowly, he told her, and she listened and what he offered seemed perfectly fine. The spread required a work hand, someone to put it into good order, look after the horses, fix the old barn's roof, the list was long. And he could be the one, as long as Cole didn't find out. Or Roose. God help them all if Roose found out!

"All right," Julia said, coming to her decision quickly. "Whatever happened in the past has little bearing on how you helped me today, Mr Nolan. When can you start?"

He came forward, beaming, "What about this afternoon?"

CHAPTER FIFTEEN

The Ranch

With his horse hitched to the rear of the little buggy, Nolan settled himself next to Julia and tried his best to appear relaxed. Inside he was a jumble of nerves, averting his eyes from every questioning glance. It wasn't until they were well clear of the town that he allowed himself a long sigh and took to studying the surrounding countryside.

"I didn't see him," Julia said without turning, her eyes set straight ahead.

"Beg your pardon?"

"The man who attacked me. I half expected to see him still lying in the street. Where d'you think he ran off to?"

"Anywheres, I guess. As far from here as possible."

"How can you be so sure?"

Shrugging his shoulders, Nolan puckered up his mouth before patting the Colt at his hip. "He wouldn't be so stupid as to try anything like that again."

"He didn't strike me as the frightened kind."

"He'll be more than frightened if he dares show his face again, I can guarantee you that."

"I think it would have been best to report it to the sheriff."

He turned and for the smallest of moments, his hand settled on her knee. Before she could react, he withdrew and sighed. "What could the sheriff do? Send out a posse?" He shook his head. "He wouldn't have the time or the inclination, believe you me."

Nothing else passed between them until Julia steered the buggy around the last bend, the vista spreading out before them, Cole's small ranch set in the midst of rolling fields, some enclosed by white fencing. In the distance, mountains formed a natural barrier to whatever it was that lay beyond. The still unchartered Territories, vast, unsettled for the most part, but an area about to be criss-crossed with the railroad, opening up America to the world.

"Roose told of problems in the North," she said, easing the buggy along the gentle incline that was the last leg of the journey to the ranch. "Tribes resisting calls to send them to reservations."

"That's all hokum," said Nolan. "It has nothing to do with reservations."

"Oh? You saying Roose has got it wrong?"

"Mistaken, maybe. Sold the lie."

"Lie? Whose lie?"

"The government's. Gold has been found in the Black Hills, and that is Indian land. The Sioux own it, but more and more prospectors and the like are encroaching in on what those Indians see as sacred. But whites don't care about that, all they care about is the gold."

"You think there's going to be trouble?"

"If the Army decide to go in and protect those same prospectors, then they will clash with the Sioux."

"Perhaps the Army won't decide to do such a thing."

"When it comes to gold, the United States government will want their share."

"You think this may have an impact on us down here?"

"It's so far away I think we can all rest easy, unless, of course, the Comanch and Kiowa copycat. Then there could be trouble."

"And Apache? Cole is tracking Apache right now."

"Apache are different, tending to travel in small groups. And they fight in different ways. Raiding, burning, looting, and ambushing. Lots of that."

A shadow fell over Julia's face, her face drawn, haggard even. Nolan studied her but did not speak. He had to fight hard to keep himself from smiling.

CHAPTER SIXTEEN

Cole

Moving across the jumbled rocks, Cole kept low, creeping forward without a sound. He had circumnavigated the place where the Apache at the far end sat, virtually buried amongst the boulders. From where he now positioned himself, Cole had a perfect line of sight. Bringing up the Henry, he squinted down the length of the barrel. An easy shot. Within a blink, the Apache would be dead, and then they could all return to the fort, licking their wounds and perhaps learning a good deal from their mistakes.

But Cole did not squeeze the trigger. He remained in his position for long, agonising minutes, whilst inside he debated with himself the best thing to do. The Apache was young, wily, no more to blame for the outbreak of violence than anybody else – white settlers included. Perhaps a show of mercy would persuade the Apache to give it up, maybe even disappear into the endless plains, move farther south into Mexico. It was a risk. Not all Apaches were the forgiving kind, but perhaps this one, being so young, might consider Cole's gesture as an opportunity to begin again. Forge a new life. One without violence.

Standing up, Cole edged closer, the Henry held hip high, his body taut like a spring, ready to go into action if the need arose.

Most could not out-fox an Apache, let alone move up behind one without being heard. Cole, unlike other scouts, had honed his skills to a high degree and, in many ways, was more adept at guerrilla tactics than the ones he tracked. A lifetime out on the plains had equipped him with a set of skills which out-classed almost everyone else. Now, standing some ten feet behind the young warrior, he stopped, again brought the Henry up to his eye, and said calmly, "Don't move, boy."

The only reaction from the Apache was a slight lowering of his shoulders, a resignation of defeat. Slowly, he turned his head and his dark eyes met those of Cole. The two stared into one another's souls.

"All I ask is you lay down your rifle and move away. I'll only kill you if you make any sudden moves."

Then something extraordinary happened. The Apache's face broke into a wide grin. "You are He Who Comes. It is an honour to be killed by you."

"But who would know?"

This seemed to cause the young Indian a flash of doubt. His face creased into a frown. He nodded. "My friends are dead?"

"All of 'em."

"And now I too shall join them."

"Only if that is what you is seeking. You have a choice."

"I have? You will spare me?"

"If you go, leave this place, make your way down south. Never come back."

"That is all?"

"That is all."

Considering his options and realising he didn't have any, the young Apache lowered his gaze, settled his rifle on the ground and stood up. "What of your other friends? They would seek my death."

Cole gestured with his own gun. "I'll say that by the time I found you, you had already gone. No one will follow you."

"Why do you do this?"

"Because I'm sick of it. The killing. I've lost count how many men I've put in the ground. It's time for me to turn away ... but if you cross me, I'll add you to my tally."

A slight smile. "I will not cross you, He Who Comes. I will celebrate you to everyone I meet."

"Yeah, well, you just make sure you do that down Mexico way."

Cole returned to the rest of the troopers, his heart heavy, unsure if his decision had been the right one. The Apache had been indirectly responsible for the deaths of too many, including young Vance. Had justice been served by what Cole had done? He knew it was a gamble. That Apache could continue with his spree of violence and bring havoc and despair to many more. Families. Prospectors. Settlers. Even soldiers. Or, as he truly believed, the Indian would take the opportunity, turn away from the violence, and disappear in a world that was big enough for everyone.

The dead were laid out in two neat rows. Troopers forming one, the Apaches the other. Standing between them was Captain Fleming, hands on hips, forlorn, deep in thought. He barely moved as Cole came up alongside.

"Anything?"

"He'd gone."

A slight turn of the head. "You didn't track him?"

"He's one Apache, on foot. In that vastness of country, he could be anywhere. I could have gone after him, but with no guarantees I would come back."

"He is that good?"

"He's Apache."

Grunting, Fleming returned to studying the bodies. "We've lost too many good men here today, Cole. I should have listened to you."

Cole's eyes settled on Vance's corpse and he could do nothing to keep the trembling from his voice as he spoke, "We've all made mistakes we will live to regret, Cap'n. Let's just pack up and return to the fort."

"There'll be an inquiry."

"And they'll find nothing to bring your command into question, trust me."

"You yourself said I should—"

Cole placed his hand on Fleming's arm. "I think we've already been punished enough, eh?" Their eyes met again and in that moment, something passed between them. A silent admission of mistakes, of the need for forgiveness.

"I'm resigning my command," said the captain, his voice strangely distant, his thoughts elsewhere.

Allowing his hand to slip away from the officer's arm, Cole did not add anything. The captain's words echoed his own feelings. The horror of the recent moments had brought home to them both how violence achieves nothing, except more violence. A vicious circle that had to be broken if this land was to become a place of prosperity and hope.

After the bodies of the soldiers were draped over horses, and those of the Apaches burnt, the survivors made their uneasy way back to the fort, all of them deep in thought, all of them defeated by the loss of comrades and the realisation that nothing had been gained.

CHAPTER SEVENTEEN

Roose

"I'll do what I can," said Sheriff Perdew, standing on the porch, looking out to the street as the townsfolk ambled by. Next to him, Roose quietly smoked a cigarette. "Your record will set you in good stead, Sterling, and I must say I am relieved. Finding law-officers out here is next to impossible and there are plenty of towns that have no one to enforce the law. I think you'll do well, and I shall endorse your application unreservedly."

"I'm obliged, Nathan. I truly am. I haven't come to this decision easily, but I feel it is the right one. I've had a belly-full of riding across the range, hunting down people for endless weeks. My job for the Army is as a scout, but all too often I've needed to shoot my gun. If I'm to do that I'd rather do it for the right reasons. Cole and me, we've both seen too much killing and for no earthly reason. I need to know I'm doing something of service, of good."

"Well, that's mighty high-talking, Sterling. Not sure if this job will supply you with such things, but it is a job that needs doing and doing well. We're lucky in that we do not have robbers and scoundrels infiltrating the lives of the good people here. On the outskirts there have been some, as you know, but this town is a good one. The occasional drunken fight on a Saturday night, maybe a wife on the receiving end of some brute's cowardly fist, minor misdemeanours, pilfering of church funds, confidence tricksters selling worthless deeds to old, confused folk. All the usual, but nothing serious. Dear Lordy, you might even find yourself bored, Sterling."

"Bored is exactly what I'd like, Nathan."

The sheriff pulled in a huge breath, puffing out his chest, holding it, then releasing it long and slow. "Must say my wife will be mighty pleased. She is forever yammering on about me getting to work around the house, fixing the place up and all. I'm thinking my retirement from law-enforcement will not be the gentle ride I hoped it might be."

"Time with loved ones is just about the most important thing of all, Nathan."

"But you don't have any family of your own, do you Sterling? You've never settled down."

"I've never found the right woman." He felt the heat rising from under his collar, because of course he *had* found the right woman. It was simply that she didn't know it yet.

"Maybe being just about the most important man in this town will bring you some wanted attention."

Sterling laughed. It could well be, or not. Either way, if things panned out the way he hoped, he could find himself sharing a life with someone sooner than anyone, including Nathan, would expect.

And Cole too.

An hour or so and two whiskies each later, a somewhat dishevelled and flustered little lady with white hair and tiny, withered hands, barged into the sheriff's office. Spluttering out a barrage of incomprehensible words, Nathan did his best to calm her as Roose looked on, slightly bemused.

"Just you calm yourself, dear lady," said Nathan, throwing a quick wink towards Roose. "Would you like me to get you something? Tea, coffee?"

"Sheriff," she said breathlessly, "I own my own tea shop so I'm not in the habit of drinking other peoples'."

"No, no of course you aren't." He pulled up another chair and leaned into her, "So tell me what all of this a—"

"I witnessed the whole thing. I thought she might come straight over and tell you, so you could apprehend that villain, but I'm not at all sure … not at all sure …"

"I'm sorry, if you could just—"

"Don't you ever wash your ears out, Sheriff! I told you! A villain, threatening her with his gun and that other young fella, knocking him down, saving the day. Why don't you know about it?"

"Because you're only just telling me now."

"You mean to say …" She looked at Roose, bewildered and confused. "I must say I would have thought … She didn't come to tell you?"

"Who didn't come to tell us what?" asked Roose, as calmly as he could. There was no point in ruffling her up more than she already was."

"Why Miss *Julia* of course."

Roose was off his chair in a blink, stepping over to the old woman, his body tense, knowing this was bound to be bad news. "Miss Julia? What do you mean? What happened?"

"She was in her buggy, having just got down to buy some goods from the merchant store, as she always does on this day. This villain, he must have tried to rob her, but I'm not sure because I only looked out once the commotion began."

"Commotion?"

"Why yes. This young fella, like I say, he helped her. Probably saved her life I shouldn't wonder. He dumped this robber, this *thief* on his backside, then brought her into my shop to calm her down. Nice looking fella he was, and Miss Julia, well I could see how grateful she was. Took a shine to him I shouldn't wonder."

"Who was he?"

"I have no idea. Young, good, open and honest face, but my, he was like hell on wheels when he put that other one flat out." She looked from one to the other. "Why hasn't she come to report it? And him? The thief, where's he at?"

The sheriff leaned back, shaking his head. "That I'd like to know."

"But Miss Julia, she's safe? Unharmed?"

"She appeared so. Last I saw her she was getting into her buggy with that nice young man beside her."

"Going back to her place?" asked the sheriff.

"That's Cole's place," snapped Roose, straightening up. "And you have no idea where this other fella, the attacker went?"

"No sir. That's what made me come over. He'd gone and I assumed he was in here, in the jail. But I can see he is not."

"So, where is he?" asked Nathan.

"I don't know."

"Seems like you might have some tracking to do, Sterling, despite what you said."

"Yeah, but first I'm gonna check on Julia."

"You think something is wrong?"

"I'm not sure. But I intend to find out."

CHAPTER EIGHTEEN

Julia and Nolan

They were skirting around the spread, Julia pointing out what needed doing and when they returned to the horses in their paddock, they leaned across the top of the fencing and gazed at those fine animals, both lost in thought.

"They are beautiful looking animals," said Nolan, not taking his eyes from the horses as they nickered and played with one another.

"I think Cole sunk most of his savings into buying them. He's thinking of setting up a stud, sell to the Army."

"Profitable that can be," said Nolan. "I know that was what Rancine was hoping to do, amongst other things."

"You don't think you'll go back to him?"

An image of Lawrenson's dead, bloated body sprang to mind, how the boulders slapped off his swollen belly as he lay in that ditch, and he shuddered. "No thank you! My days of working for that miserable old shyster have ended. I'm working for you if you'll have me."

He turned to her and she quickly looked away, cheeks reddening. He returned to the horses and smiled.

"I never know when Cole will be here," she said distantly. "He's forever scouting for the Army, and living here, so alone and isolated, so far from town, I have to admit I get frightened."

"I'm sure you're safe."

"Maybe, but even so, on a cold, crystal clear night I hear the coyotes howling and I wish there was someone with me."

"Well, you have Cole."

"Cole is not the settling down kind. He's been kind to me, I cannot argue about that, but he is not the most *loving* of men, if you get my meaning."

"I think I do." He turned and leaned back against the fence. He stared at the log cabin, a yellow glow seeping from the open door. A place to settle down in that was for sure. "He sounds to me like he's a man who doesn't appreciate what he has."

"You could be right. He often spends time at his father's spread. My, that is one impressive house, but there is something between them, a distance that prevents Cole from moving in. He's a restless spirit. Perhaps that is why he scouts."

"I have heard he is a dangerous man."

"Oh yes, he is that."

"And his partner, what of him?"

"Partner? You mean Sterling?" Nolan nodded, careful not to be too eager. "He comes by every now and then. Sterling is nothing like Cole. He's warm, kind-hearted, always asks how I am, if there is anything he can do to help."

"Perhaps he is a little in love with you?"

That reddening grew deeper. "Mr Nolan, you should not be so personal. Sterling Roose is a gentleman, and he would never—"

"I apologise, Miss Julia," said Nolan quickly, pushing himself off the fence to look at her with deep, sincere eyes, "I have insulted you and that was not my intention. Please forgive me."

"There is nothing untoward between Sterling and myself. Nothing at all."

"No, no, of course not. I did not mean ... Look, let me accompany you home, make sure you are safe and then I shall pay my leave."

"You don't have to. It's just that I'm ... Living out here ..." She stroked away an unruly lock of hair. "It can be so lonesome. Sterling is kind, but he would never ... He and Cole, they go back years."

"Yes, I understand."

"Perhaps when it is time for me to move on … But that is wishful thinking."

"Is it? You have plans to move on?"

"Cole has made it clear he does not want a relationship. He was only giving me safe haven. His words, not mine."

"I see."

"Do you?"

"You're hoping that when you do finally move on, Sterling will accompany you. Is that it?"

"Perhaps."

They fell into silence until, quite unexpectedly, Julia gave a heavy sigh, linked her arm through Nolan's, and walked him back to the cabin.

"I'll make you supper," she said.

"I'd like that."

He smiled, but the outward one was nowhere near as big as the huge one developing inside.

Sometime later, with the sun just beginning to dip down below the horizon, Nolan set out for the town of Paradise. Things were developing well, now all he had to do was settle his account with Caine. A good friend, Caine had no place with his plans, however. Shapiro would not take kindly to an outsider being au fait with the robbery, so it would all have to be taken care of. This was real heartbreaker for Nolan. He was fond of the young cowhand. They shared the same attractions and their private moments had been some of the fondest Nolan had ever known. Perhaps not quite as fond as the moment he had just shared with Julia, but close enough. However, business was business and the ends needed to be tied off. He rode with a grim resolve, but with a wide grin on his face. Memories of Julia stirred through him and he looked forward to the next time they were together. Telling her some details of the plan proved not so difficult after all. True, he had left out the part where Cole and Roose would die, but she seemed more than amenable to joining him after the robbery. What passed between them after supper, the urgency of it,

72

the unleashing of so much pent-up lust ... Such thoughts lightened his mood and he rode in a sort of daze.

So lost was he in his thoughts that he failed to see the single rider hidden behind an outcrop of large, jagged rocks. It was arguable he would have noticed the rider anyway, for he was a man of great skill and stealth. Nolan rode, and the man watched and when Nolan was well out of sight, the rider turned his horse and headed towards Julia's isolated cabin, his face set hard.

She was just trimming the candles when she heard the footfall on the veranda outside and froze, wondering what to do. It could be anyone, of course, but at this time, so late? As she stood rooted to the spot, pondering, the tension mounted. The bar was across, so whoever it was couldn't burst in. She had time. The Henry was above the door, and the Wells Fargo Cole insisted she keep in the bedside cabinet drawer. Both weapons seemed like an impossible distance away, but she knew she would have to choose one.

Struggling to calm her pounding heart, she told herself it could be Nolan, back to reassure her that what he had told her in the height of passion was not really true. The story that he had sought her out for her own sake, not as some part of his hair-brain plan to murder both Cole and Roose and so ensure that the town was easy pickings for the bank robbery, which was to come. Could that be it? Could it be that Nolan was, as he told her as they lay on their backs in the bed she shared with Cole, a changed man, that she had captivated him, made him want to strike out on a different path?

She jumped in fear at the sound of the impossibly loud knock. Waiting, she held her breath, gazing wide-eyed at the door.

"Julia, are you in there?"

She gaped, hardly daring to believe who had spoken. "Sterling?"

"Oh, thank God, I thought perhaps ... Open the door, would you? I need to know you are unharmed."

With shaking fingers, she swung away the bar and eased open the door, gasping when she saw the wild, frightened face of Sterling Roose.

Without a word, he wrapped himself around her, holding her tight for several long minutes.

"Sterling," she said into the thick material of his coat, "let me go, you're suffocating me."

"Oh God," he said and released her, instantly putting his hands on her shoulders. "I'm sorry, but I was so worried when I found out what had happened."

"What had happened?"

"Back in town. The attack."

Stepping aside, Julia bade Roose to enter, then shut the door behind him, swinging into place the bar. Sweeping back that same unruly lock of hair, she frowned at his concerned look. "Sterling, it's all fine." She strode passed him. "Can I get you some coffee?"

"No, I haven't ... Julia, who was that man, the man I saw leaving just moments before I arrived?"

She felt her spine grow rigid. With her back to him, swilling out the coffee pot, she nevertheless imagined what his face would be like. Accusing. He knew. He'd seen Nolan and now she had a simple choice – to lie or come clean. She turned around. "Oh. He was, *is*, the man who helped me."

"Helped you with what?" He moved closer, "Julia, I thought I recognised him."

"Did you? I don't see how, he's ... Sterling, why don't you sit, and I'll make us some coffee, then we can talk." She gave him her most disarming smile, but it didn't appear to work this time. The Army scout stood ramrod still, studying her. She became acutely aware of her attire: the dishevelled nightdress, her lack of under garments, her wild, unkempt hair, which Nolan raked through with his fingers, urging her to yield. And she had. And Roose could see it, his smarting eyes, flickering with tears, speaking all of his inner thoughts.

"Who was he?"

A shrug before returning to the coffee. "As I told you, the man who helped me. I was attacked. An attempted robbery. He came to my aid, that is all."

He was with her, turning her, his fingers digging into the soft flesh of her biceps. "Sterling, you're *hurting me!*"

"I said I recognised him. I know now who he is."

"So, what if you do?"

"It was Nolan, wasn't it? The scoundrel who laid me out flat in the jail, almost broke my skull. And now you and he ... Oh dear Lord, Julia. What have you done?"

"Don't be so childish," she said, swatting away his hands. The anger welled up, uncontrolled. "All right, yes, it was Nolan! So what? It's not a crime to invite inside the man who has saved your life."

"Saved your life? From what?"

"I told you – I was accosted, threatened. A gunman, demanding I give him all my money and Nolan, he was there, to help me."

"Just like that?"

"What?" She stopped, not able to understand his point, the anger too great, blinding her reason. "What do you mean by that?"

"Convenient he just happened to be there – the man who clubbed me unconscious and allowed you to break Sergeant Burroughs free."

"He did no such thing!"

"And Captain Phelps, what about him? He died and you were the one blamed for it all. But it wasn't you, was it, as Cole and I both suspected. Was it Nolan? That's why he ran isn't it?" His eyes burned. "Tell me – *was it him?*"

"You're insane, Sterling. None of this is true."

"So why did he hightail it out of here? Looked pretty darn guilty to me."

"There was never any evidence – and even if there was, no one can prove anything. Sergeant Burroughs was the guilty one, the one stealing Army horses and selling them to the Mexicans."

"All right, then you explain to me why Nolan suddenly just showed up, straight out of the blue. Explain it."

"How dare you! I don't have to explain anything to you."

"No, and you won't even explain the real reason why he was here tonight." His eyes dropped and roamed over her body. "I can see very clearly what that reason was, Julia. Very clearly."

She struck him across the face with such force he reeled backwards, stunned. "Get out," she screeched. "Get out of my house, you filthy, despicable—"

Clutching his face, Roose forced a laugh, "*Your* house? I wonder what Cole will make of that after he learns about your little tryst!"

"Get out. Get out now!"

Without another word, Roose did so. Even more than the stinging across his face, it was the stinging in his heart that brought the tears to his eyes.

CHAPTER NINETEEN

Nolan

He dismounts some way off and takes a moment to settle himself. It is late, the evening well advanced now, and he is certain no one has seen him trot up to the entrance to the town cemetery. Readjusting his gun belt – although he has no plans to use the Colt holstered at his hip – he ties up the horse at the gate and moves along the narrow path that winds its way to the top. The neat rows of simple crosses with their simple inscriptions reflect the starlit night from their white surfaces and the glare sends a curious shiver through his body. He has never liked cemeteries, and as he walks, he remembers how he stood next to his father's grave, tears rolling down his cheeks as he watched them lower the rough-hewn coffin into that terrible, black hole. He could have sworn he heard the old man shouting, 'Let me out, let me out!' Now, here he is again, not as a mourner this time, more a purveyor. Of death.

Caine steps out from the deepening night and he is rubbing his ribs and looking more than a little angry.

"How you doin'?" Nolan says.

Caine gapes at his friend. "How am I doin'? A little tap, you said, nothing that will hurt, you said. Well, it hurts, and it hurts like sin!"

"I had to make it look realistic. Anything less she would have suspected."

"I reckon you did it because you wanted to."

"Ah, hell, Caine, don't be so—"

"Because you enjoyed it."

"That's just nuts!"

Nolan takes the chance to look around him. The night has, by now, engulfed everything and there is not a soul – living or dead – that is anywhere close. Nevertheless, he cannot shift the feeling that unseen eyes are watching. Eyes from the graves, eyes which are accusing, cursing him. He shivers and Caine notices. "You see, you know it's true."

"It's not that, I just don't like this place is all."

"Then why'd you choose it? Seems to me you don't know what you're doin' lately. Your brain is all scrambled and seeing that beauty in that buggy I can understand why."

Caine steps closer.

"No, no, that, *she* has nothing to do with any of it."

"Don't lie to me! We had a good deal going, you said. She has money, money we could steal then set up for ourselves up in Wyoming. That was what you said."

"And that's what I still mean to happen, Caine. You and me. Just as always."

"Are you sure?"

"Yes, I'm sure." And to underline his sincerity, he places a hand on his friend's shoulder and squeezes it. "You and me."

"All right." He gives a tiny giggle and rubs the side of his face. "You sure can punch when you want to, I'll give you that. I don't ever want to get into a fight with you."

"Then it's good we're still friends."

"Yeah, you're right. I'm sorry."

Nolan lets his hand slip from his friend's shoulder. "I'm the one who should be saying sorry."

"Well, let's just put it down as part of the deception, okay."

"No, I really mean it. I'm sorry. You were always so good to me."

A slight tensing of Caine's shoulders, a sign of his confusion. "Eh? What do you mean?"

Nolan half turns, swinging his body in a sharp arc, the knife in his hand slicing into Caine's body, thrusting upwards, under the rib cage, through vital organs, piercing the lungs. The power of the blow is enormous, and he grunts with the force of it, but it is Caine who makes most of the noise. A sharp, high-pitched squeal, whether through pain or surprise Nolan cannot tell. He plunges the knife farther still and they both topple over the nearest cross and land with a solid thump to the ground.

Caine's eyes flash bright in the darkness and Nolan sees the anguish there, the sadness. Betrayed. Murdered by the only man he has ever loved. Nolan sees it and he holds the blade deep, deeper and deeper still, the point rupturing the heart and he sees the brightness blink into nothingness.

He stands and he looks.

And then he weeps.

CHAPTER TWENTY

In the Night

Unlike the sound of Sterling's insistent pounding, this knocking is quiet, tentative and she has the time to take the Henry from its place and engage the lever. "Who is it?"

"It's me."

His voice is strained, almost as if he is in pain and she almost throws the rifle aside in her desperation to open the door to him and take her in his arms. She sees him, the light from the nearby oil lamp casting him in an unearthly shade of sickly yellow. But it is not this which grips her attention, unwilling to let go. It is the blood. He is awash with it and his face is as pale as a corpse.

"Oh, my dear Lord," she cries and would hold him if it wasn't for the fear of being covered in all that gore herself. She takes his hand and draws him in. He shuffles forward, like one in a trance, and she guides him to the table where he sits and stares.

Stooping down beside him, she grips his hand and peers into his lost, vacant eyes. "What has happened? Was it Sterling? Oh, dear God, don't tell me he followed you and—"

Shaking his head, he turns to her and although his eyes remain lifeless, he manages a thin smile. "Roose? No, although he will be after me now. No, it was the man who attacked you."

"But you said he would be arrested, that he would—"

He presses a finger over her mouth, a finger filthy with dried, black blood. "Ssshh, my darling. No. He must have escaped because as I rode to Rancine's, he waylaid me. We fought and I ..." He looks away and his body convulses. "It was *horrible,* Julia. Like something out of a nightmare. The way he screamed and ran at me."

"What did you do?"

Another convulsion and he held himself, wrapping his arms around his own body as it shook. "He was strong, full of rage. We fell to the ground and we twisted and rolled. His knife, big, heavy, like a sword, but I managed ... I don't know how, but somehow, I ... It went into him, so frightening the way the blade slid inside him, with no resistance."

Regardless of the blood, Julia slowly lowers her head onto his lap and one of his hands massages her scalp. "Oh, my love ... They will come for me now. No matter why it happened, no matter it was my life or his, they will come for me and Roose will lead the hunt because he wants me dead. For what happened this day, and for what I did to him. His revenge."

Lifting her eyes to his, she knows it is the truth. Sterling would never forgive. It was not in him to make such a gesture, to let the past go. He would track Nolan down and string him from the nearest tree. She has no doubts.

"What can we do?"

His face grows taut, eyes staring to something very far away, and he shivers more violently than ever. "I haven't been honest with you, my love. And I need to be. This night, and what has happened, if there is any good to come out of it, then it is my confession to you."

"Confession? I don't under ... What is it you need to tell me? You have already told me so much."

"I need a drink first. Whisky. Have you any?"

Without a moment's hesitation, she goes to where Cole keeps his bottle. She pours a generous measure into a misted glass and brings it back to the table. Nolan is sitting bolt-upright in his chair, his hands flat on the tabletop, and his eyes stare into the distance. As soon as he sees the Bourbon, he seizes it and throws it down his throat, gasping as he winces. Immediately, he holds out his hand with the glass, gesturing for another and she goes back and fetches the bottle. With her eyes never leaving his face, she takes a chair and sits next to him. The second drink he takes much more slowly and, between sips, he tells her.

"I did tell you some things, but I am not sure how clear it all was. I returned here to trap you, Julia. To trap you into taking me in, but I needed a reason. The reason was Caine. We set it all up, the attempted robbery, my being there to help you. I was then to come back here and take all of your money." He pauses and looks at the way her eyes fill up and something stabs at his heart. "But as soon as I saw you, I knew I could never, ever do anything to harm you. I knew it when I first saw you all that time ago, but of course I buried it, not wanting to believe it. The very moment I saw your face again, all thoughts of swindling you, they disappeared, because in that moment I knew I loved you."

Shaking her head, a tear slips down her cheeks, and her lip trembles. "Oh ... Oh my..."

"And I know you feel the same. Tell me you feel the same."

More than her lips trembles now and he reaches out to hold her hand. She does not pull away because she knows it is true. She has wanted this for so long. A man to love her, not use her. Yet, all of this has happened so fast. Can she be sure, can she allow herself to believe that someone could come into her life the way he did and give her all that she craved? His deceit, his plan to take from her? How about that. If he could do such a thing, then what else could he do? These thoughts, and so many more, skirmish across her mind, but the need for him blows away all her doubts, together with her common sense. "Yes," she says quietly, and he leans into her and his lips brush against her. "Yes, I do."

She watches him ride away knowing he has things to do, knowing that as soon as the daylight returns, they will find Caine's body and Sterling will add everything up. Time is against them, but she trusts Nolan enough to let him go and make his peace with Rancine. This is what he has told her, and she agrees. There is no point in having more than those two scouts hunting them down, for she knows Cole will join with his friend. So, if they can work it right, Nolan will return with money and fresh horses and they will ride south, into Mexico, and their new life will begin.

She leans her head against the door jamb and smiles. He is all she has ever wanted. Yes, he has killed, but what choice did he have? His honesty and his loyalty make her breathless. Life has been so very cruel, but now she has the chance to put it all behind her. Cole never offered her anything except a roof above her head. Yes, she is grateful, but her needs are so much more than four walls could ever provide. Nolan has given her a glimpse of what life can truly hold and she is determined not to let it slip from her grasp. As she turns away to start packing up her few belongings, her heart is pounding, no with regret, but with excitement and contentment. She might even allow herself to think she is on the verge of happiness.

Sleep does not come. She is overly excited with the prospect of starting a new life. So, she makes coffee and sits on the porch, despite the cold, and tries to work things through in her mind.

Any solutions or answers, or any clearing of doubt, do not come easily. She rocks gently in the rocking chair, both hands wrapped around the coffee cup. The wind is getting up and with it comes the cold. A glance skywards and the whiteness of the sky brings the knowledge that snow will soon be falling. At this time of year that could be the precursor to a blizzard and travelling in such is not something she relishes.

But they will have to go.

She cannot stay here any longer. Roose, his manner was so ... *unusual.* Where had the mild-mannered, softly spoken man she had always known disappeared to?

What was it he said which has caused her mind to twist and turn ... Ah yes, something about Nolan turning up 'out of the blue'? She has to admit, here in the quiet with no distractions to befuddle her still further, it was strange the way Nolan seemed to appear just at the right moment. And the story about him running away after what had happened at the jail. He helped her to set Sergeant Burroughs free, but in so doing laid Sterling flat. The sudden, unexpected violence of it shocked her then, and now, with the way Nolan had pummelled her attacker ... although she is grateful, it all seemed too neat, too contrived. As she rode away with Burroughs, her memory of that dreadful moment grows clearer. Captain Phelps, hands above his head, Nolan's gun pointed directly at him. She did not hear a shot as she made good her escape, but she did learn later that Phelps was dead, that everyone believed it was either her or Burroughs who had killed the captain. Could it have been Nolan? Was he capable? Of course he was! His original plan was, as he said, to rob her. Might he still carry that through? Surely, his confession meant he was honest, that he had had a change of mind. He loved her. Didn't he?

Confused, but also resolute, she decides to go into town, settle her bill at the merchandise store, perhaps speak to the little old lady at the teahouse, thank her, reassure her. Then, returning here, she will leave Cole a note and that will be that. Setting aside her worries, her concerns, her mind is made up at last. She drains her coffee, gives the sky one last glance, and goes back inside to make herself ready.

CHAPTER TWENTY-ONE

Cole

They cross the expanse of the plains in silence, travelling through the night, their thoughts blacker than the darkness. Cole, at the head of the ragged line of broken, defeated horse-soldiers, concentrates on the way his horse's hooves blow up tiny dust devils with each step. In the night, the land appeared white, the recent snowfalls making no noticeable change to the uniform greyness of the earth. Sustained downpours of either snow or rain would need to fall for months for any green to reappear. Perhaps it might happen, but not this night. The wind, a mere ghost of what could be, barely ruffled the mane of his horse. Above him, the sky is cloudless, the stars twinkling as if they too mocked him. He should never have come on this journey. He should have refused the order and gone back to his ranch, to Julia, and made some effort. If effort he could gather. No matter how hard he tries, nothing stirred within him when it comes to her. A vibrant, attractive woman and yet there is something, something he cannot fathom. He knows Sterling feels an attraction. No fool, this knowledge brings little concern, nor the tiniest spark of jealousy. This fact alone makes him realise that Julia is not going to find a place in his heart. Is it her former deeds, her readiness to kill? Could he even trust her?

Would there come a dark night, such as this, when she will plunge the knife deep into his heart?

Stirring as a horse sidles up next to his own, even in the night light, Cole catches the captain's haunted look. "I guess we should camp soon, even if only for a few hours."

"If that's what your orders is," says Cole.

"Yes. I suppose so."

"It can only be for a few hours, though. Our cargo is going to be a little ripe if we delay our return."

"Dear God, you're all heart, ain't you."

Cole stiffens and for a moment he is about to remind the captain that if it weren't for his inept handling in the way he went about bringing the Apaches in, none of this would have happened. A good many more wives and mothers would not be crying into their breakfasts for the next hundred days or so. But he doesn't say such things, her lets it go, allows his shoulders to relax, grunts and wheels his horse away to help set up camp.

He sleeps, but it is unsettled and as the first streaks of dawn cross the endless sky, he sits up and stretches out his back. He feels like a million ants have walked across his eyes and he rubs them vigorously with his fists. If only they had found a place close to water and camped by a stream. He needs a wash. Badly. Instead, he decides on using his canteen, calculating they will all be back at the fort before the thirst really kicks in. But even as he starts to soak his neckerchief with water, he senses something isn't right and when the trooper out on picket duty comes rushing into camp, everything is confirmed.

"You better come and see this, Cole. Quick."

Strapping on his gun belt, he follows the quivering soldier across the broken scrub, wondering what awaits but knowing, from sheer instinct, it is going to be bad.

It's worse than bad. It's just about the worst it can get, and Cole sinks down onto a nearby rock and gazes in disbelief at the sight before him.

"What are we going to do?" wails the young trooper.

"You hold his legs and I'll cut him down."

Captain Fleming swings from the sturdy branch of one of the few large trees growing in that otherwise barren place. Perhaps that was why he chose this area to camp? Who could tell? Certainly, the captain would not be telling anybody about it. He is dead and Cole wonders what he will write in his report about this disastrous of all expeditions. The truth simply will not cut it.

CHAPTER TWENTY-TWO

At Shapiro's Hideout

Riding without stopping, Nolan makes good time, taking a direct route because he assumes, rightly as it turns out, that no one knows the position of Shapiro's hideout.

At the entrance to the deserted gold mine, a swarthy, big-bellied man stands chewing on a cheroot. The Winchester he carries is looped over one forearm and his eyes flicker left and right, forever watchful.

Nolan sees the man from a distance and slows down to a gentle walk, raising his hand as he calls out, "Don't shoot, it's me – Nolan!"

The big man is already going into a crouch as he calls back into the depths of the mine for his boss to come out and see who has arrived. The Winchester, now snapped up to his face, is unerringly focused on Nolan.

"Ah, my good friend," says Shapiro as he emerges out of the darkness of the mine. He is accompanied by several others, all hitching up pants or stuffing in shirts. The dawn is barely an hour old and they look dishevelled, grumpy, riven with curiosity.

Edging forward, Nolan puts up both his hands and does not drop them until Shapiro claps his hand on the big-belly's back and sniggers. "Relax *amigo*, this must be good news."

As the gang gather around, Shapiro orders coffee and grits to be made ready. Dismounting, Nolan waits until Shapiro steps forward and puts his arm around Nolan's shoulder. The gang leader leads him over to the remnants of a small fire that Big-Belly used to warm himself through the night. "Get some more wood on this," Shapiro shouts and one of the men hastens to do his bidding. At a nearby outcrop of rock, Shapiro sits and beckons for Nolan to do likewise.

"I have news."

"I hoped you might," said Shapiro. "I must be honest, I was thinking that maybe you had forgotten about us."

"No way. Not with the bank being so full."

This welcome news causes Shapiro's eyes to twinkle with delight and he reaches over and embraces Nolan enthusiastically. "I knew you would not let us down. I always had faith in you, unlike the others." He releases himself and, grinning, checks that someone is making the coffee. Satisfied, he returns to Nolan and grins again. "Tell me, what is this news?"

"They're dead."

Shapiro's mouth falls open and for a moment a silence like a heavy steel door falls down over them, shutting everything else out. "What? You mean ...?"

"In the end, it was easy. They were drunk, celebrating some hunt they had been on. Indians. I snuck into Cole's log cabin and did for them both." He pats the heavy-bladed knife at his hip. "They knew nothing about it."

"That is a pity. I would have liked Cole to have suffered. He made a fool out of me. I am disappointed."

"I didn't really have much choice."

"Log cabin you say?" Shapiro is rubbing his chin, eyes distant. "At Cole's spread?"

Nolan nods his head, averting his eyes from Shapiro when his boss frowns at him.

"You know I went there once."

Now it is Nolan's turn to gape. "To Cole's place?"

"Yes. After I broke free of that damn prison, I intended to go there and kill him myself. It was empty. Deserted."

"He doesn't often go there."

"But this time he did? To a tiny ranch he has no time for?"

Nolan squirms. He cannot help it. Shapiro's eyes study him with an intensity unlike anything he has ever known. Perhaps he suspects and if he does, then Nolan will have to end it all here. It would be touch and go, with his gang so numerous, but not all of them are armed. If luck is with him ...

"I told you," Nolan continues, keeping his voice calm, steady, "he was sleeping off a drunk."

"With the other one?"

"Sterling Roose, yes."

"And you killed them?"

"Yes, I did. Why in the name of sanity would I tell you otherwise, Shapiro?" Hoping this show of anger will divert any more suspicions, Nolan jumps to his feet, fists clenched. "I want that money as much as you do, as much as we all do!" He swings his arm around in a wide arc to indicate the rest of the gang, all of whom are dead still, watching. "The bank is open and ready for taking. Just as you told me to make it."

"I did not think you would be able to kill them. Are you sure no one else will be suspicious? The town sheriff, perhaps?"

"He's a fat old man, not worth a dime. It's safe, Shapiro. We can ride in and shoot up the whole town without anyone brave enough to lift a finger."

Another silence. Icy this time. Shapiro appears to be going over everything Nolan has told him, sifting through the words, convincing himself of their veracity.

"What's the matter, Shapiro? Don't you believe me?"

A long sigh slips from Shapiro's thin, cruel mouth. "I must, *amigo,* because nobody would be foolish enough to lie to me."

And then came the grin, lighting up his face, dispelling the charged atmosphere in an instant. Shapiro stands, embraces Nolan again, and calls to his men to gather around. "We have plans to make, and bellies to fill!"

Someone produces a half bottle of tequila and they all break into laughter.

"It's a little early for that, isn't it?" Nolan looks dubiously as the bottle is handed over to him.

"It is never too early for tequila," says Shapiro, "especially when we have so much to celebrate – to our dear departed friend, Reuben Cole!"

Urged on by them all, Nolan takes the first mouthful and creases up his face as the liquid fire hits the back of his throat.

Later that same afternoon, the third bottle finished, Shapiro kicks one of his men in the leg to rouse him from his slumber. Rubbing his eyes, the man squints upwards to his boss and smacks his lips.

"Check he is unconscious, then ride out to Cole's ranch. I want confirmation."

"Eh?"

Shapiro wants to punch the man struggling to his feet, scratching at his crotch. "I want *proof*, you half-wit. Once you have it, you get back here as soon as you can."

"But boss, I thought we were heading into town to take the bank? Before you got us all drunk, that is."

"You do as I say," snarls Shapiro and juts his chin towards the man who is swaying unsteadily before him. "Check out the cabin and bring me the news I want to hear." Then, taking a breath, he leans towards the man's closest ear and gives him the directions. "Now go, and whatever happens do not be seen. By anyone, you understand."

"Yes, boss."

"Good, now get!"

CHAPTER TWENTY-THREE

Discoveries and Confessions

A cold wind blew in from the west, battering hard against the huddle of men who stood in the cemetery looking down at the blood-spattered corpse at their feet.

"I'm getting too old for this sort of thing," mutters Sheriff Perdew with meaning. His face, ashen, appears drained and haggard. Old before his time, possibly sick with something ravaging through his withered body. Roose stands next to him, and doesn't know what to make of him. He doesn't know what to make of the corpse either. He says so and the sheriff throws him a filthy look. "Murder is what it is."

"I know that much," says Roose and gets down on his haunches. Although the morning is moving on, the cemetery remains eerily dark, as if reluctant to give up the night. Having already had a good look outside the entrance, Roose now inspects the ground. "The murderer made off on foot, down through the gate to where his horse was waiting."

"You can catch him?"

"Certainly. But he'll be desperate, so I'll need at least two more men. Or I can wait for Cole."

"Best do it now rather than later. He may well already be out of the Territory."

"Could be." Roose stands up and stares at the body for quite some time. "Anyone know who he was?"

No one is forthcoming until a lanky youth with buck teeth and a thatch of bright orange hair steps forward. "Could be one of them drovers from the Rancine ranch."

"You know him?"

"Not directly," says the youth. "I do recall his face."

"It is a face to remember," says the sheriff. "More like that of a girl. Or angel."

"Well, if he's one of them he's found his way back home, I would suspect. But yeah, his face ..." Roose frowns. "This could be an argument gone bad, not premeditated, so it could be even harder to solve. I'll take myself across to Rancine's before I set off to find the killer. But it ain't gonna be quick."

"Just another reason for me to put in my badge," says the sheriff.

Some of the men chuckle but Roose takes the comment for what it is – an invitation. This is his chance and he means to take it.

As the group of men start to disperse, someone says, "I'll fetch the undertaker," and the sheriff, wheezing loudly, sits down on a nearby stone tomb, fashioned in the shape of a coffin. The irony is not lost on Roose. "You already settling in, sheriff?"

A scoffing bark of a laugh follows. "You can joke about it, Sterling, but I have to tell you, I don't feel too good. And with this cold weather coming..." He lets the comment hang there, unfinished. He looks up as he gathers his coat around his throat. "I'm feeling my age, that's the truth and if it wasn't for the fact that I'm ..." He stops. "Are you all right, Sterling?"

But Sterling is far from all right. Searching every corner of that lonely place, he slowly pushes his hat back from his brow. "There's one thing I almost missed."

"You never miss anything as far as I can tell."

"That's as maybe, but ... I'm wondering, Sheriff ... where is this dead man's horse?"

. . .

93

Bringing the buggy to a slow, easy halt, Julia climbs down and surveys the street. It is mid-morning, but the cold wind bites hard. Well muffled in thick coat, gloves, scarf, and bonnet she still feels it. There will be snow. Travelling will be hard. Why have the fates conspired to make everything so difficult?

Securing the horse, she steps up onto the boardwalk and clumps down towards the merchandise store. It is warm inside and she breathes a sigh of relief. Mr Stanley, the proprietor, stacks up a big, pot-bellied stove in the corner and he beams when he sees her. "Why, Miss Julia. How are you this somewhat bitter morning?"

"I am well, thank you Mr Stanley. I have come to settle the bill."

"Oh." He looks stunned, but soon his face wrinkles up into one of pure joy. Rubbing his hands, he dips behind the counter and begins to leaf through a large, thick ledger. "It's a piffling amount, Miss Julia. Cole almost always settles it whenever he gets back from one of his trips. Is he home again?"

"No, not yet." She opens her small purse and extracts the required amount. He does not bother to count it and she likes that. In another world, she could take on the management of such a store as this, fill it out with everything anyone from around those parts could ever possibly want and need. "Thank you, Mr Stanley, for all your past service."

"Oh. Well, I ... you know, it's all in the ... Are you going someplace?"

"Yes ... for a little while. Thank you again."

A brief smile followed by a furtive glance around the shop. There is nobody else.

The shopkeeper tilts his head, puzzled. "There is something else you were wanting?"

"Yes. Reuben – Mr Cole, I mean. He gave me a Wells Fargo, for personal protection, but I'm not very well-schooled in its use. I have heard there are better options."

"Indeed, there are, Miss Julia. That little Colt Navy is old-fashioned, uses powder, cap and ball."

"Might you have something a little more ... *effective?*"

"A Peacemaker is probably the best bet, Miss Julia. It's not so very big and uses cartridges, so it can be rapidly reloaded." He ducks down below the counter and returns with a shiny walnut box. Easing it open, he waves his hand across the contents. His cheeks puff out. Obviously proud of these wares, he beams towards her. "I have to confess; I do not get that many ladies inquiring."

"Is that it?" She points at a bright and shiny revolver sitting snug in a bed of plum-coloured velvet.

"That's top of the range, with ivory grips. There is a cheaper version, just as effective."

Sucking in her bottom lip, she gives herself a few moments to consider her options. She could continue with the Wells Fargo, but she wants her own revolver. She knows how to shoot, has done so on many occasions, and what she is planning might mean using up more than one cylinder's worth of bullets. "I'll take it," she says, lifts it and weighs it in her glove hand. "It's heavy."

"And reliable."

Smiling, she pushes the required amount across the counter and then she is gone, stepping outside again in the raw, bitter weather, her pocket sagging with the weight of the Colt.

A few flakes of snow are floating down from a sky almost uniformly white. Shivering, she dashes along the boardwalk to the little teashop on the corner and goes inside.

A bell above the door chimes cheerfully and almost at once, the little proprietor appears through a beaded curtain. "Well I never," she cries, clapping her hands in genuine glee. "I was only just thinking of you, my dear. How are you? Do please come inside, sit yourself down. I'll make you a nice, hot cup of China tea."

"No, no," she says and holds up a gloved hand, "I'm only here to ... to tell you. All is well and I am perfectly recovered."

"Yes, well, thank goodness is all I can say."

"Yes. It was traumatic, to say the least, but—"

"Thanks to that young man, is all I can say – he saved the day."

"Yes, he did! Thank goodness he was here. Could I ask..." She steps closer, checking the shop for any other customers, even though it is clear there are none. "You saw the whole thing, I suppose?"

"Well, I was here, in the shop, heard the commotion and all ..."

"Yes, but the young man, the one who helped me? You saw him?"

"Yes. Of course, when I stepped outside after he had—"

"I mean before."

"Before? Before your attack, you mean?"

"Yes, did you see him standing anywhere close? Loitering I suppose you could call it."

"Not that I can remember, I was in the back, you see, preparing everything for lunch time and I could not see much from where I was—"

"I did," comes a voice from beyond the curtain. "I saw him." Parting the beads, a thin, angular looking woman, as grey as the proprietor, but considerably taller, appears. She dries her hands on a checked tea cloth as she steps forward.

"This is Sylvie," says the old proprietor. "I'm Noreen, by the way."

"Thank you," says Julia with a smile. "Sylvie? Is that French?"

"I am Canadian," says the new arrival as she folds the cloth over her arm. "I moved here with my family some years ago, but yes, we are French."

"Sylvie makes the most delicious cakes," puts in Noreen proudly. "I've never tasted better."

"I'm sure your customers feel the same," says Julia then, the niceties done with, she grows more serious. "Tell me what you saw please, Sylvie."

"The man you speak of, the one who helped you? I saw him talking with the one who tried to hold you up."

For a moment, Julia cannot speak. It is as if a huge, icy cold cloud has enfolded around her, smothering her. Her breathing grows laboured and she reaches out for something to stop herself from falling. Hands help her, grip her by the arm and gently lower her into a chair.

"Brandy," says Sylvie simply. She drops to her knees, hands clasping Julia's own. "I am sorry, madam. This is a shock."

Mumbling, unable to form words, Julia stares into the face of the French-Canadian. Noreen appears with a small glass in her hand and Julia takes it, sips, coughs, but instantly feels better. Blinking, she holds onto Sylvie's hands. "Are you absolutely sure?"

"Yes, I am afraid so. I did not think anything of it, at the time, but after the attack I went to the sheriff to tell him."

"But he did nothing."

"He did not seem all that interested, saying the matter was sorted out thanks to the other man's intervention."

Nodding, Julia drains her glass and hands it back to Noreen. "Thank you. So, they knew each other."

"There is more," said Sylvie. Julia looks at her and notices a tiny tremor running across her eyes. "I also heard what they spoke about."

CHAPTER TWENTY-FOUR

Roose

T he body lay stretched out upon the undertaker's table. Having cleaned up most of the blood, the gaunt looking man in black suit with tails who conducted the preparations of the body, thrust out a crumpled piece of paper towards Roose. "It was in his shirt pocket. I took a look, thought you would be interested."

Taking it with great care, Roose unfolded the paper and read the scrawl. Each word grew larger as he took them in, emotions ranging from startled disbelief to, by the time he finished, desperate urgency. "How long has he been dead?"

"Can't say," replied the undertaker. "I ain't no doctor, but the rigor has passed, so I'd say at least twenty-four hours, maybe less."

Grunting, Roose whirled away and went outside. He mounted his horse and kicked it into a gallop, heading into town and the sheriff's office, all the time his mind filled with the enormity of the dead man's written words. The only part he was uncertain about was the timing. Whoever had murdered him must have got into a dispute over the plans, but what that dispute could be he had no means of knowing. Possibly how the loot would be shared out? And if the murder had occurred the previous day, the robbers could be heading into town at any moment.

Reining in his horse outside the office, he jumped to the ground and was mounting the steps up to the door when it opened, and two people stood there.

He gaped, sucking in his breath at a rush. "Julia?"

"Hello Sterling," she said, her lips trembling as she spoke.

"Roose," said the sheriff, who stood next to Julia, face set hard. "We have some news, and it ain't good."

"I know," he said, brandishing the paper. "Is this it?"

The sheriff took it and read through it quickly. "That's about the size of it. The gang is coming in to rob the bank, and they mean to have you and Cole out of the way when they do it. I'm old, Roose. There is no way I can do this on my own, and the town just hasn't got the manpower or the grit to see this thing through."

"Sterling." Julia stepped forward, taking one of his hands in hers. "I've been a terrible, blind, stupid fool."

"No," he said, unable to keep the tears from gathering under his bottom eye lids, "No, you haven't. It's my fault. I knew you were unhappy, and I should have ..." Shaking his head, he tore himself from her grasp, straightening his back, gritting his teeth. "Where is he?"

"He said he was going to the Rancine ranch. It's where he used to work."

"Dear God," said the sheriff. "Surely Rancine would not be involved?"

"In the robbery? No, I doubt it." He gave Julia a withering glance. "Did he say anything about this to you? Who he was in cahoots with?"

"No, not a word. Sterling, I didn't know anything about this, I promise you! He talked about us going away, starting a new life but never anything about any robbery, or what he intended to do to you and Cole. I swear it."

His eyes held hers for a long time and he could see the sincerity there, but it still hurt him to know what she had done. Sharing her bed with a man she barely knew, and he ... He having feelings for her for so long. And for her to contemplate ... contemplate what? His and Cole's death?

"I didn't know about any of that," she said as if she could read his thoughts. She moved closer and took his lapels in her hands and for a moment Roose believed she was about to shake him. "We have to find him, stop him, and then we have to set a trap for the robbers. We *must,* Sterling. It's the only way."

She was right, of course. Anything she had done, mistakes, misjudgements, call them what you will, had to be pushed aside. What mattered now was stopping Nolan and his gang, if indeed it was his gang. "You're right," he said and smiled. He saw her face change, soften, and then her lips were brushing against his chin. He stepped away, his stomach turning over, not sure how to react. His feelings for her were not changed. "I'll ride out to Rancine's. If Nolan is still there, I'll apprehend him, bring him back. Then we can start to make preparations."

"Be careful, Sterling," she said.

He left with those words emblazoned on his mind. Words which he would never forget.

CHAPTER TWENTY-FIVE

The Ranch

S haking his head, the sheriff looked at Julia as if he were in pain. "I'm not so sure if that is such a good idea."

"I need to be there when Cole returns, to let him know. Hearing it from someone else wouldn't be right."

"But you can tell him here!"

"No, he'll go straight to the ranch. He always does. Nobody at the fort will know what has gone on here, so he'll follow his usual path. I'll go back, wait for him."

"And what if this Nolan character is there? What if he has not gone to Rancine's? What if—"

"Sheriff, the world is full of what-ifs. If Nolan is there, I'll deal with it." Julia hadn't told anyone about the Colt in her possession, but she now unconsciously stroked the pocket where it lay. "I'll be fine."

"I'll come with you, just in case."

"No, I told you, I'll be fine. Trust me. If Nolan is there and he sees you, he'll spook, make a break for it. God knows, he'll probably kill us both before we got within a hundred yards. Cole's Henry is still above the door."

"All the more reason why I should—"

She gripped his hand. "It'll be all right. Besides, you need to organise some sort of defence. Maybe get the bank tellers out of there, lock everything up, apart from the safe. Clear it out and leave the door open." She caught the sheriff's perplexed frown. "We need to shock them, Sheriff. They are going to ride in here thinking it's going to be as easy as getting drunk on the fourth of July. If the town can't stop them with gunfire, then at least we can make it as difficult for them as possible when they come stumbling outside again, wondering what on earth is going on."

"Yes, yes you're right. But please, you must ..."

A simple squeeze of his hand and she was gone, marching across the street to her buggy. She gave a tiny wave, then left the town at a steady trot.

She made good time, following the ancient track out of town, the way she had always come, but never with so much trepidation. The enormity of the situation burrowed into her very heart and soul. Nolan. Everything he'd said, the words, promises, all of it so many lies. He'd preyed on her vulnerability, and all in order to convince her to abandon Cole after luring him from town. Was it also Nolan's plan to ambush Cole and perhaps Sterling as well, to kill them and make the robbery of the town bank so much easier? She cursed under her breath as memories of the moments she'd spent with Nolan flashed across her mind. What a fool she'd been, swept off her feet so easily! Such thoughts only served to make her more determined than ever to thwart him. Make him pay. Yes. Not only had her pride been damaged, but her dignity too. She did not know if she had it in him to kill him, the way she had killed Sergeant Burroughs, but she knew she needed to confront Nolan and show him that his lies had not worked. And more. Show him how devastated she was with his deceit.

The ranch appeared as she had left it. A lonely place, not even the few horses cantering around their fenced field lifting the solemn, oppressed atmosphere of the place. She wondered, not for the first time, why she stayed? Perhaps that was why she had jumped so eagerly at Nolan's invitation? Alone in a lonely place. Was nothing more calculated to send her deeper and deeper into a trough of depression? What Nolan offered was a way out. A chance. But he'd lied, using her for his own purposes. The hatred boiled over. She took out the Colt and studied it before placing it in a canvas bag. She urged the little buggy forward.

———

He'd arrived a little before her, gun drawn, checking the rooms. As the silence continued, he realised that Cole and Roose were not there. No signs of struggle, no upturned chairs, tables. No blood. Nolan had lied. He'd tricked Shapiro. For what ends, he could not fathom. Maybe to buy himself time, to double-cross them all, murder them and claim the reward money. Better than a cut from the proceeds of the bank raid. It could be. Shapiro alone was worth what, five thousand dead or alive? That was a lifetime's worth of money. If the bank held a sizeable amount, how much could Nolan hope to take? Two thousand at the most. Yes, that was it. It had to be. He'd turned bounty-hunter on them all.

The sound of approaching hooves spurred him into action. He rushed through into the little back room and out through the door. The cold hit him like a fist and, with one hand around his collar, and the other on his gun, he crouched down against the rear wall and waited.

From the other side, he could hear the buggy stopping, the hand-brake going on, the sound of her boots hitting the ground as the driver jumped down. It was all so very quiet. Like the grave. The thought caused him to shudder.

From inside, the door crashing open, a female voice crying out, "Cole? Cole are you here?"

But of course, he wasn't. Was she aware of Nolan's double-cross? Her voice was tremulous, rattled. Then came the sobs and he decided to move, edging around the side to the open door. He stood in the doorway and watched. A beautiful woman, head down, tears dripping from the tip of her nose to the tabletop. He could have stood and watched her for a long time. Instead, he crossed threshold, easing back the hammer of his gun as he did so.

CHAPTER TWENTY-SIX

Cole

Second-Lieutenant Morris stood, mesmerised, as Cole dismounted. "What has happened?" he asked, trailing his eyes over the horses laden down with their dreadful cargo. Bodies wrapped in white sheets or blankets. Cole merely shrugged.

"They ambushed us. Took out a lot of our boys. The Cap'n, he ... Well, let's just say he's amongst those of us who lost."

"But, his wife. She sent a cable telling us she's coming. To join him."

Taking in the young officer's bewildered look, Cole swallowed down the tiny cry trying its level best to burst out of his mouth. What was he supposed to tell her? It would be down to him to do so, the one surviving officer in the troop. "I'll meet her. Let her know." He blew out his breath. "Get a detail to take the bodies away, Lieutenant. Get them ready for burial. But not these boys," he indicated the bedraggled, dishevelled survivors. "They'll need to be left alone for quite some time."

"I'll see to it, sir."

Nodding, Cole tramped across to the drinking hall. Then a bath. There was no way he could ride out and see Julia in the state he was in. She'd never speak to him again.

He went to the bar and drank, his eyes staring into nothing, wishing to God he had the power to turn back time, or at least the guts to have told the captain not to go down into that ravine. Despite the whisky, or perhaps because of it, he knew this was going to be his last duty. Julia would be relieved, he knew that much too. To see her face lighting up as he told her, that would be everything. He would make the effort, show her the care, yes, the love, to make her feel at home with him. That was what mattered now, more than anything else.

In the upstairs rooms, he lowered himself into the hot bath he had ordered before his whiskies. Luxuriating in the sweet-smelling bath oils, he put his head back, draping his legs over the end. Closing his eyes, he allowed himself to drift, the tension immediately draining from his muscles. Unable to fight against his weariness, he slipped into deep sleep. Within seconds he was snoring.

Persistent and rough, someone somewhere shakes him into consciousness.

"*Cole! Cole, wake up!*"

Eyes springing open, Cole sat upright, blinking in his confusion. A man is there, tall, wide across the shoulders, a face lined with worry.

Sterling Roose.

"What's...?" Suddenly becoming aware of how cold the water is, Cole placed both hands on the bath's rim and hauled himself to his feet. Wrapping his arms around his chest, he shivered violently. "How long have I ...?"

"Never mind that," spat Roose. "Get your clothes on and meet me downstairs. We have a situation."

With only time for a swift gulp of coffee, Cole follows his friend out into the daylight. "I just got back from Rancine's," says Roose as he strides across the empty parade ground to where two saddled horses are waiting. "They told me a few things, all of which fit together to make up quite a picture of our friend."

"Sterling," says Cole, grabbing his friend by the arm. "What are you talking about?"

Grimacing, Roose rounds on his friend. "Nolan. He's planning on robbing the bank at Paradise. Originally, he was going to murder both you and me, until Julia put it all together."

"Julia? Sterling, I haven't a clue what you are talking about."

So Roose tells him. Everything, including what he'd learnt from Rancine. How it must have been Nolan who had murdered one of the main cowpunchers there, then murdering a young cowboy up at the cometary, the young cowboy who Nolan had employed to attack Julia. Everything. Julia's suspicions, how she found out what it all meant, and the note which confirmed everything. Cole listens, body gradually turning to liquid. Weak, disorientated, it takes him some time to make sense of it all. Some of it makes him want to be sick. Why would Julia sleep with Nolan? This, the most devastating part, causes him to die a little inside. "Dear God," was all he can manage.

"Listen," says Roose, ignoring his friend's obvious pain, "I'm going into town to help the sheriff organise things. You get over to your place and make sure Julia is all right. Bring her back into town. She's not safe out there on her own. If Nolan was to come back ..."

"Yes," agrees Cole weakly, putting up a hand, "yes, I understand Sterling."

"Are you going to be all right yourself?"

"I'll be fine."

Not at all convinced, Roose swings himself into the saddle. "Be as fast as you can. None of us know who Nolan is in cahoots with, but it must be a gang of at least half-a-dozen. They won't be expecting the reception committee I'll put in place for 'em, I can guarantee you that."

Nodding, Cole strokes his horse's neck for some considerable time while he watches his old friend ride out through the fort gates.

It's as if his entire world has been cut out from underneath him. Why would she do that? All right, he may not be the most garrulous of people, never giving her any intimation of his feelings, his hopes and plans, but even so ... Dragging in a shuddering breath, he pulls himself into his saddle and gently steers his horse through the gates. Roose is already little more than a black smudge on the horizon, galloping hard in the direction of Paradise. Cole's ranch is in the adjacent direction and it isn't going to get any closer unless he moves himself soon.

Wondering what he will find, Cole finally spurs his horse. With every pounding step, his determination grows. Soon, a hardness returns to his limbs, the queasiness all gone. Resolved to do whatever is required, Cole rides with his back straight, his jaw set solid.

CHAPTER TWENTY-SEVEN

At the Ranch

Looking up, a tiny gasp from her lips, Julia stared into the dark eyes of the stranger. He was grinning, the gun in his hand unwavering.

"My, oh my, *señorita*, how pretty you look." He stepped fully into the tiny room.

Julia did not flinch. In a strange, inexplicable way, she had been expecting someone, if not this particular man, to come. Ever since she learned the truth about Nolan, what he was planning, she knew there would have to be some sort of reckoning. So, although this man's sudden appearance frightened her, she was prepared. On her lap was the canvas bag containing the Colt. She bided her time, watching the little man edging up to the table.

"Where is Nolan?"

A small swallow before she answered. "I don't know."

He tilted his head to one side, frowning. "I don't believe you." Scanning the room, he chuckled. "Has he killed them?"

"Them? You mean Roose and—"

"Roose and *Cole*, yes! Has he done it?"

"Of course he has. I suspect even now he is riding back to your hideout. If you go now, you will catch up with him."

The man's smile turned into a grotesque leer. "Nice try, my pretty one, but I do not think Nolan is going anywhere, except to Hell."

He paraded himself around the room, picking up items, opening a drawer in the writing desk under the shuttered window, which he opened and stared out into the surroundings. "He has some fine horses," he said with his back to her. "You tend for them while he is not here?"

"Yes. Among other things."

"Yes. I can imagine." A wry chuckle. "Where is he?"

"I told you, Nolan, he—"

"Don't *lie to me*," he screamed, whirling around to face her, the gun coming up in his hand.

His eyes dropped as he centred on the Colt Peacemaker in her hand. His grin broadened.

Then she shot him.

The blast sounded incredibly loud in the small confines of that small room. Thrown back against the window, he stood, gaping, disbelief etched into his features. He watched her as she eased back the hammer to fire a second shot. This act seemed to reanimate his senses and as she fired again, so too did he.

This time, the combined blast sounded even louder.

CHAPTER TWENTY-EIGHT

The Camp

Shapiro returns from his prolonged vigil, standing on a high outcrop to observe and signs of his man's horse. Now he goes to the campfire, fills a tin cup with bitter coffee and drains it, throwing the dregs into the fire. His eyes roam across the assembled men. Some are cleaning their weapons, other checking their saddles. Nolan sits a little apart, whittling away at a thin piece of wood. Shapiro readjusts his gun belt and moves towards him. "Tell me again how you killed them."

Nolan stops, the blade halfway across the wood, and he stares into Shapiro's face. "What did you say?"

"You said you killed them. Cole and his friend. How did you kill them, *amigo?*"

"I told you. They were drunk. I killed them as they were sleeping."

"Yes, but I ask you again ... *How?*"

Nolan swallows hard. With a violent swipe, he cuts his knife through the wood and throws it to the ground. "What is this again, Shapiro? Don't you believe me?"

"I am just curious, that is all. You used that," he points at the knife in Nolan's fist. "You cut their throats maybe?"

"As they were sleeping, yes."

110

Shapiro pulls a face. "It is not so easy to do that." He emphasises his point by running the fingertips of one hand sideways across his own throat. "There is a lot of what is called cartilage there. And ligaments. It surprises you that I know so much, eh? You have to saw through it all, like you might a piece of wood." He cackles and allows his left hand to drop down next to his holstered pistol.

"Not if you get it right here," says Nolan, jabbing two of his fingers into the carotid artery of his neck. "You cut that, then it is goodnight time."

"And that is what you did, eh?"

"Yes."

"Just like that?"

"Yes. Just like that." He emphasises each word, his eyes never faltering. Shapiro is measuring him, looking for a flinch, a blink, anything that would put a doubt in his mind. But Nolan remains impassive. Cold. "They were drunk. I did Cole first, as he is the most dangerous, then Roose. I don't think they even knew."

"Blood."

"Eh?"

"There must have been lots of blood. I remember I shot a man in that place," he jabs at Nolan's artery, "and the blood, it came out like a waterfall. Blood red waterfall." Another smile. "So how come when you came here to tell us, you had no blood on your clothes."

"I changed them."

"Ah. Where, at Cole's cabin?"

"Yes."

"Then you came here directly, is that it?"

"Correct. Shapiro, if you have something to say why don't you just—"

"And your knife? You cleaned that too? Your boots? Your hands? All cleaned. Plenty of time to clean all of that, yes?"

"Obviously, as they were dead, and I didn't think they would be—"

"And the woman?" Nolan stops and blinks. Shapiro's eyes widen, together with his smile. "Cole has a woman, yes? Where was she while all of this was happening?"

"I didn't know he had a woman."

"No? Are you sure, *amigo?*"

"Of course I'm sure. Why would I ..." His voice trails away as he stares in horror at the small, silk handkerchief Shapiro dangles in his hand. Embroidered around the edge is a red motif in the shape of a heart.

"You recognise this, *amigo?* It was in your saddle bag. Whilst you were sleeping, I went through your things. I found this, and inside, a note."

"You sonofa—"

Before Nolan can react, Shapiro's gun hand moves in a blur and suddenly, Nolan is facing the barrel of a Remington Army, hammer cocked. "Her little note is very touching. You may think I am an ignorant Mexican, but I know my letters well. She loves you deeply, so I am thinking you have made a little deal with her. A deal that might include Cole, eh? So, please, no more nonsense. I want the truth, *amigo*, or I put a bullet in your brain."

Three of the gang drag him to a nearby tree. They strip him and now he waits naked, shivering in the freezing afternoon air, as they lash his wrists together with leather thongs. Shapiro stands and examines Nolan's knife. Then he snaps an order and, attaching a rope to the thongs, they throw one end over a branch and hoist Nolan into the air, where he dangles, arms high above his head, shoulder ligaments stretching. He is screeching and the sound reminds Shapiro of the pigs his mother kept when he was a little boy. So long ago. Like a dream.

"Now, boss?"

Shapiro smiles and nods.

The crack of the bullwhip brings even happier memories.

After he told Shapiro everything he needed to know, the gang leader orders his men to saddle up. As they rush to obey, Shapiro takes a moment to squat down next to Nolan's quivering, bloody body. "Know this," he says softly, "when we return, we will bring with us your woman. I shall feast on her and you shall watch. Afterwards, when you see how happy and contented she is, I will kill you. Until then," he pats Nolan's cheek, "stay well."

Laughing, he swaggers away.

"Darius," he barks and one of the gang looks up, frowning. "You stay with him. Make sure he does not die."

"But boss, I want to—"

"If he dies, so do you!"

Crestfallen, Darius stomps away from his horse, head down, mumbling something.

Meanwhile, Shapiro singles out two others. "Take the trail to Cole's ranch. I want no mistakes this time. Kill him."

Shapiro wheels his horse in the direction of Paradise, lifts his hat and waves it like one possessed. "Ride, *muchachos!*"

With much hollering and slapping of horses' rumps, the gang pile out of the camp, every one of them grinning with the expectation of the thrills to come.

"You must drink," says Darius, kneeling down beside Nolan. He offers him a canteen of water, which Nolan gulps at thankfully. "Not so fast, my friend. You do not want to choke to death." He cackles.

Revived a little by his drink, Nolan props himself up on one elbow and stares into the man's face. "They have gone?"

"Yes, my friend," sneers Darius, lifting the canteen to Nolan's lips again. He smiles as Nolan drinks. "That's it. When you can sit up, I shall make us something to eat." He sighs and looks into the far distance where a spreading cloud of dust is the only evidence of the gang's departure. "I wish I was with them."

Grunting, Nolan wipes away the sweat from his eyes with the back of one quivering hand. He studies Darius or, more accurately, the way he wears his rig. Cross-bellied, grip facing his right side. The closest side to Nolan.

He almost smiles at the man's stupidity.

In one flowing movement, Nolan whips out the gun and puts two quick slugs into Darius' guts. The man screams and is blown backwards where he writhes on the ground. Meanwhile, Nolan tries to sit up. The pain in his back, where the bullwhip bit so deeply, causes him to seize up solid and he stifles his own scream through gritted teeth. Giving himself a distraction, he turns his attention to Darius flaying around, bent-double, hands clamped to his stomach. "Darn it," breathes Nolan and shoots him through the head.

Silence descends and Nolan thanks God for it.

CHAPTER TWENTY-NINE

The Ranch

I t looked like something out of a faraway land, gripped as it was by winter. The snow had settled, casting everything in a comforting white blanket. At least from a distance. The air, however, almost burned the throat it was so cold. Reining in, huddled in his coat, and watching, Cole knew there was something wrong as soon as he spotted the horse tethered at the side of the barn. It was a horse he did not recognise, the rig jet black, studded with jewels, not something anyone he knew would ride. Slipping from his own mount, he drew the Henry repeating carbine from its scabbard and moved down the slight incline leading to the cabin, keeping himself low. Darting from one measly piece of cover to the next, his boots crunching through the snow. In the eerie silence, the sound echoed all across the valley and he felt certain that at any moment someone would appear, guns blazing.

Nobody did. Cole crouched down behind a freezing boulder, exposed to the very fiercest of chilly blasts of wind, and engaged his carbine. His face tingled with a myriad of tiny needles forever stabbing at his exposed flesh. If he was forced to remain outside in the night, he knew he would not see the morning. The sun was already low in the sky and he calculated less than an hour of daylight remained. Taking a breath, decisions made, he charged from his cover and zig-zagged towards the open doorway.

Not slowing down, he rushed past Julia's buggy, causing the tough little pony to buck and whinny loudly, and continued up the steps to the doorway. He summersaulted through the opening, hoping to catch whoever was inside unawares. He did not know who to find, but he knew it would not be Roose. If someone was holding up Julia, then retribution was close. Maybe it was Nolan. God help him if it was.

The first sight which confronted him was that of a dead gunman, crammed under the open window, eyes staring into nothingness. Punctuating his body were two huge holes, black with dried blood and, next to him, a gun. That can only mean one thing.

He turned his head slowly, praying he would not find anything, that whoever it was who had killed this man was long gone.

Cole was not a man used to praying. Faith, belief, call it whatever you will, these were not concepts he understood nor had ever bothered with. Perhaps he should because now, looking across the room, he saw her, lying in a crumpled heap, the blood in a wide pool around her, and for a long time he did not have the courage, nor the strength, to move.

She was dead. That much was plain, even from where he sat he could see that, and as this realisation hit him, the tears came. If he had shown some hint of his feelings for her, then perhaps none of this might have happened. He knew nothing of what had transpired, but he knew something terrible had. Creeping over to her, the sobs racking through him, he gently lifted her head into his arms and cradled her there. The bullet had struck her in the throat, her life's blood a deep, dark stream cascading down her bodice. She was so cold in his arms. So cold ...

Later he stood on the porch and smoked a cigarette, the plume of blue smoke mixing with his steaming breath. He watched the sun go down and he knew his life was turning a new page. Julia, gone, his unspoken love drifting away on the wind, along with his heart, now as frozen as the winter landscape.

He did not know how long it would be before the thaw came.

CHAPTER THIRTY

The Robbery

The sun was nothing more than a dim smudge when the riders came into town, muffled in their thick blanket coats, hats crammed down hard on their pinched faces. They all wore gloves and scarfs, but the cold penetrated into their very flesh making them slow, weary. At their lead, Shapiro scanned the streets. He did not expect to see anyone this early and his plan was to find the nearest saloon, wait until the bank opened at nine, then hit it with everything they had. After he had checked, of course, that Nolan's words were true.

With two men left standing outside, stamping their feet, Shapiro went through the batwing doors of the Parody Hotel and Saloon, three of his gang behind him, all of them groaning in ecstasy as the heat from the twin wood burners positioned in the far corners hit them with a heavy blast.

From somewhere a frail looking man, bent over with age, appeared carrying a full pail of steaming water in one hand and a mop in the other. He pulled up sharply as he set eyes on Shapiro and his men. "Oh Lordy," he said.

"We need coffee," snapped Shapiro, pulling off his coat. Around his waist were two guns, butts turned forwards, and across his chest a bandolier bulging with cartridges, ending in a shoulder holster. The others, similarly armed, settled themselves at a large, round table, stretching out their legs and blowing out great streams of air.

"We ain't open yet," said the man, his voice shaking, as were the cleaning things in his hand. He settled the bucket down before it slipped from his grasp.

"You is now," snarled Shapiro, drawing one of his guns to underline his point. "Coffee."

Without a word, the little old man scampered behind the counter and disappeared into a room beyond.

"What time is it," asked Shapiro to nobody in particular as he holstered his gun.

"Beats me," said one of his men. "Too darn early that's for sure."

"It's just gone six-twenty," said one of the others, the proud owner of a silver inlaid fob-watch that he kept on a chain across his ample stomach. He snapped the cover closed and dropped the fob to its home in his waistcoat pocket. "That gives us two and a half hours to kill."

The others groaned.

"Best if we relieve Tweedy and Ramon," said Shapiro, leaning across the counter to find a half bottle of whisky on the shelf there. Grinning he pulled out the stopper with his teeth, spat the cork away and took a slug. Gasping, he studied the liquid inside the bottle before shooting a glance towards the others. "Tell 'em to come inside."

As one of the men did his bidding, Shapiro turned and leaned back against the bar, eyes closed. Two and a half hours ...

Another man came through the rear door, still dressed in nightshirt. He took one look at Shapiro and gaped. "Gentlemen," he began, stepping closer, "it is not usual for us to—"

"Just get the coffee," said Shapiro in a bored voice without looking at the man, "or else I'll kill you all and set fire to this stinking old shack of a place."

Instantly the man, sensibly deciding not to argue, disappeared without a word into the back room.

The batwing doors opened, and the others came in, rubbing themselves briskly. "It is so cold out there!"

"Warm yourselves by the fire, boys," said Shapiro, taking another drink, "we have plenty of time."

"It's as quiet as the grave outside," said one of them, moving across to the nearest wood burner, palms outstretched.

"Just as I like it," said Shapiro and closed his eyes once more.

Pushing the little old man out the back door, the big owner whispered, "Tell Roose they is here."

"You do remember what to say, don't you Lawrence?"

"Of course I do. Now scat!"

The old man scurried off with the speed of a worn-out old tortoise. Lawrence sighed deeply before returning inside and set to preparing the coffee.

He threw the body of the gunman out into the open ground, knowing that as soon as they felt safe enough, the buzzards would be making quick work of him. Naturally, he took more time with Julia, washing away the blood, even combing her hair before he lay her down upon the bed. Stooping close, he kissed her gently – something he had never done while she was alive – and covered her with a blanket. Then he went into the room and did his best to tidy up, cleaning the blood, which almost turned his stomach. Perhaps he caught an hour's sleep, but he soon roused himself, despite his joints aching and the tears stinging his eyes. Forced to break the ice that had formed on the surface of the washing bowl, he threw water over his face and felt a little revived. Nothing, however, could expunge the image of Julia's corpse, images that simply would not go away.

Outside again, he took several deep breaths before unhitching the buggy. He took both the pony and the dead gunman's horse into the paddock to join the others. When he returned, after prioritising Julia's burial, he would take the animals into the barn where they could spend the cold nights.

Normality, he knew, would soon return.

Together with the loneliness.

Sometime later, with the morning advancing, he rode away not knowing what to expect, only that at some time soon, Nolan and his men would ride in and attempt to rob the bank. Roose would have done his job, of that Cole was sure, and he could not stop himself from grinning at the prospect of what was to come.

The loud snap of the fob-watch cover closing made them all jump. "It's just after nine."

Shapiro, who had been dozing in the far corner beside the wood burner, sat up, yawned, and stretched luxuriously. Automatically he reached for the whisky bottle standing on the floor next to him. Finishing it, he stood, rolling his shoulders, easing out the cramps in his muscles. He eyed the bartender arranging glasses and bottles behind the counter and sauntered across as his men checked their weapons for the umpteenth time. He looked at his right hand, the forefinger and thumb misshapen and he flexed and unflexed them, wincing a little. "You're certain Cole is not around?"

The bartender turned, his face serious. "Like I told you, rumour has it he got himself killed on his last outing against some Apaches."

"And Roose?"

"That was nasty, and the sheriff is out investigating even now. Over at Cole's ranch. He left late last night and has not returned."

"Nasty in what way?"

"Woman came in here like a startled hen, screaming that there'd been a fight at the cabin and Roose had been shot. I don't know anymore."

"Sounds convenient."

"Convenient or not, I believe it's the truth."

"If it turns out to be drivel," said Shapiro, leaning across the counter and seizing the barkeep by the collar, "I'm coming back for you, *amigo*."

The man's jowls wobbled as he spluttered, "I'm telling you as it was told to me."

With a hefty shove, Shapiro let the man go then swung around to face his gang. "Keep your wits about you, boys. We hit the bank hard and fast."

They all fell in behind him as he stepped outside.

The chill wind hit them all instantly. Pulling his collar tight around him, Shapiro strode out onto Main Street, head snapping left and right. There was no one. Not a soul. Not even a horse. It had to be the cold, there could be no other reason why this place had suddenly become little more than a ghost town.

If Shapiro all but knew it, there was a simple reason. Sterling Roose, if not the architect then the executioner of the plan, stood in the livery stables, deep in the shadows, watching the gang striding by. He could strike now, gunning them down in a blaze but Cole, who had ridden in a little under an hour ago, held his arm and gave a single shake of the head. "Wait," was all he said.

So, they did, grinding their teeth, anger boiling over at the sight of the gang's arrogant swagger.

"How many you count?" asked Roose.

"Six. There'll be a seventh back at the saloon, with the horses. He'll bring 'em up to the bank as soon as the shooting starts." He drew in a deep breath, becoming concerned. "But Nolan isn't among them."

"That worries me. He could be waiting somewhere, as a back-up."

"As leader, he'd be there, right at the front. Anything else and the others wouldn't follow."

"So, what are you saying? That Nolan isn't their leader?"

"I reckon it's the one at the front. I know him from somewhere, but I can't quite fix him in my mind ... He has something about him, a presence. He's their boss, I'm sure of it."

"And Nolan? Where's he?"

A blinding light instantly blazed in Roose's eyes and, snapping his face around to face Cole, he uttered through gritted teeth, "Julia!"

Roose went to move, but Cole caught hold and pulled him back into the shadows. "Don't be a fool! If they see you, they'll figure it's a trap and ride out of here like the hounds of hell were after 'em."

"But we can't just—"

"We get this done first," said Cole, his grip tightening. He had not yet told Roose the horrors of what had transpired back at the ranch, knowing his old friend would already be racing off to see for himself. He needed to convince him that all was well. "Nolan's gone, Sterling."

"You can't be sure of that."

"What would it profit him to harm Julia?" He had to turn away as renewed tears threatened to spring forth. "Come on, let's get into position and get this thing done."

They rushed through the main door, Winchesters ready, covering the whole interior of the bank.

"What the ...?"

Nothing but a cold, empty space glared back at them. No tellers, no customers. At the counter where clerks would sit, chairs waited empty underneath, papers stacked, pencils sharpened and ready. But nobody to do anything.

One of the gang vaulted over the counter, kicked in the manager's office door, and stood, breathing hard. With his back to them all, he gasped, "There ain't no one here."

Another, lifting up the hatch this time, strode towards the massive, green painted safe and groaned. "Boss, this is open." He swung around, pale faced, lips quivering. "It's been cleaned out."

A dreadful drumming had been growing in Shapiro's ears and now he whirled away, clamping hands to the side of his face. "No, no, no," he blared, not wanting to believe any of it, hoping that once he opened his eyes, he'd find himself back at the hideout, all of it a dream. A nightmare.

"Boss, what in the name of Almighty are we gonna do?"

Bringing his face up to meet every one of his terrified gang, Shapiro slowly gathered himself, overcoming the disbelief, the dread. "Nolan. He's double-crossed us, gave the town warning." Both hands came up, curling into tight fists. "I'm gonna rip out his lungs. *His lungs!*"

Striding towards the door, a charging bull out of control, he reeled out into the cold, ignoring it, barely conscious of how quiet the street was. More than quiet. Deserted. Brandishing his arms in a wild cartwheel, he signalled to his man at the saloon, roaring at the top of his voice, *"Bring the horses!"*

Through a shimmering haze of hate, he thought he saw something. Something that shouldn't be there, not now, not in this dead, barren place. Even as his men spilled out all around him, he still could not believe it. Until that is the vision was so close there could be no ignoring it.

"You," he managed, his voice nothing but a drizzle of something he never wanted to be a part of again. Defeat.

Before him, the vision stopped, nonchalant, detached, almost as if it were the most natural thing in the world for him to be there. For it was a 'him'.

"Hello Shapiro," said Cole.

Stepping out from behind the far side of the bank, Roose held a twin-barrelled sawn-off shotgun in his hands, the Remington in its holster and another in his belt. He was glad he had so much fir-power because from where he was standing, the bank robbers were also well tooled-up. All of them were facing Cole, unaware Roose was at their rear. Once the shooting started, if they chose not to lay down their firearms, it was going to come as a huge surprise to them all.

Cole was speaking, his voice calm, as it always was. "You boys all put down your guns and place your hands on your head. There ain't nothing for you here, so quit now while it is still looking good."

For a reply he received a huge, scoffing guffaw from Shapiro who, even though his own voice was trembling, made out he was as uncon-cerned at seeing Cole there as he would be at finding a bird flying over-head during a walk in the countryside. "And so speaks Mr Reuben Cole. Boys, this here is the great Army scout of the Territories, a man who took away my freedom and who I have sworn to kill."

"The only person who took away your freedom was you."

"Ah, yes, you would say that, wouldn't you Cole, to disguise your own dishonesty. Whatever happened to the money we took from that bank, eh Cole? Where did it go?"

Shifting his weight to his left leg, Cole frowned. "It was returned. As always."

"You know it was not. And now this bank, empty. By who, I wonder?"

"You talk too much."

"Ah, touched a nerve, eh? Well, not to worry. There are six of us my friend. It is for you to throw down your guns. Then, it will be just you and me." His teeth flashed in a nasty looking snarl.

As his men tensed and prepared themselves, a voice broke out from behind them. "I'd take it real easy, boys," said Roose.

A sudden mood change fell over the gang, one of uncertainty charged with fear. Men turned their heads and, realising the odds were now evened out, shuffled and grumbled.

Shapiro quickly responded, his voice taut with tension. "We're moving out boys. Steady does it and keep yourselves ready."

"Give it up," said Cole. "I can't allow you to walk away from this."

"You are not a lawman, Cole. You have no authority."

"He ain't," said Roose, "but I am, and I have all the authority that is needed. I'm acting sheriff and I'm ordering you to throw down your weapons."

Hesitating, the gang members looked from one to another. "What do we do, boss?" asked one of them.

"We'll take you in," continued Cole, "and those of you who ain't wanted we'll let go again. That's a better deal than dyin', boys."

"It is you who will die if you do not let us ride off," said Shapiro, waving his arm again at the horse-holder outside the saloon. "We shall meet again, Cole."

"No. We won't. You're a wanted man, Shapiro. The bounty says one thousand, *dead* or alive. I'm not a bounty hunter but I can't deny that sum would set me up real comfortable for quite a while."

"I would die first."

A tiny smile trickled across Cole's mouth. He nodded towards Shapiro's hand dangling next to his holstered gun. "Looks like you've been doing some practising."

"You destroyed my right hand true enough but I've had years to learn to do just as well with my left. You'll find out soon enough."

"Your call."

Shapiro made it, flinging himself to his right, hitting the dirt in a roll as his gun came up in his left hand, the pistol spouting smoke. Behind him, his men also went for their own guns and as Cole veered away, Roose opened up, hitting two of the men with the shotgun, sending them screaming to the ground. Fanning his gun as bullets filled the air, Cole winged two more. He made it to the boardwalk and crouched down behind a group of stacked barrels adjacent to the merchandise store. He drew his second pistol and laid down evenly spaced shots into the gang as they fumbled around, firing wildly. One went down, hit in the chest, and Roose joined in, the shotgun discarded, both hands filled with his Remingtons.

Meanwhile, amongst all the smoke and noise, Shapiro sprinted across the street, signalling like a lunatic for the horse holder to arrive.

From his cover, Cole watched it all. The horse holder was now riding up, a string of horses behind him. Shapiro swung himself up into the saddle and loosed off two or three shots in Cole's direction, all of which went hopelessly wide. Ignoring them, Cole sprang forward and shot two more gang members, dumping them in bloody heaps. Without a pause, he swept up one of the gang's fallen Winchesters. As he brought it up to his eye, he looked deep into Shapiro's face, that irritating smile on the man's face. Next to him, Roose was on the ground, clutching at his leg. This wasn't good. There were others still standing.

A loud whoop from Shapiro snapped Cole into action and he whirled around, working the Winchester frantically, emptying the rifle into those gang members still standing.

A bullet zinged past and he fell to the ground, bringing out his last loaded gun but knowing the range was too great. He fired nevertheless as Shapiro struggled to bring his horse under control. He wasn't winning, the horse in a mad frenzy, spooked by the close proximity of so many bullets. The man next to him was faring better and as he kicked his horse into a gallop, Shapiro roared out his frustration.

From his position, Cole had a clear view of the situation. He knew he must take up another Winchester and shoot Shapiro down.

As things turned out, he didn't need to.

From the narrow gap between two buildings, old Sheriff Perdew stepped out, the shotgun shaking in hands which were either too old or two weak to hold it up. Or perhaps it was the fear. Whatever, he managed to bring up the gun and emptied both barrels into Shapiro's body, blowing the gang boss sideways across his horse. Some of the spread struck the animal, not fatally but enough to send into an uncontrollable charge. Shapiro, one foot caught in the stirrup, went with it, his body bucketing and bouncing down the street to disappear into the distance.

Cole watched, horror-struck. All around him were groaning and bleeding men, one of whom was Roose, holding onto his leg as the blood frothed through his fingers. Desperately, not even giving himself time to stand up, Cole rolled over to his friend and held him tightly. "Oh, dear God," he said.

"I'm all right," said Roose, his face white with pain. "Help get my tie around it, stop the bleeding as much as you can, then get the doc. But hurry, Cole, hurry."

It was bad, this close Cole could see just how bad. His stomach turned to mush and turned over. He twisted himself around, screaming at Perdew to fetch the doctor, then he ripped away Roose's tie and applied the tourniquet. He pulled it as tight as he dared, and the blood flow lessened. A tiny flicker of hope ran through Cole's body, but the greyness of his friend's face meant the fear remained. All he could do now was wait. And pray.

Something like a boulder the size of anything found in the Rocky Mountains presses down on his chest and he no longer possesses the strength to lift it away. Instead, Shapiro lays on the ground, forcing himself to breathe, each inhalation and accompanying exhalation ratcheting up the pain.

Something blocks out the sun. A shadow, a figure, he knows not which. The pain is his world now. Nothing else exists.

"You're in a bad way, boss," says a voice. It sounds a long way off but is crystal clear. "I don't think you is gonna last out the next hour. That old guy, he done paid you the Lord's dues."

Shapiro wants to speak, but he cannot voice anything out of throat so dry it has completely closed over. Instead he groans, wanting to tell this man, who he thinks is one of his gang, a man called Tweedy, to take him away, bury him, burn him, anything that will prevent Cole from claiming the bounty. The final ignominy.

"Me," says Tweedy, looking back towards the town, "I'm gonna finish you off now, boss. End the pain. Then I'll claim the bounty. No one will recognise me when I bring you in, telling them I found you out on the plain. You're gonna make me rich, boss. That's about all you have ever done for me, you lousy piece of horse dung." He grins and pulls out his gun, wraps his hat around the barrel and presses it against Shapiro's head.

Shapiro wants to move, squirm away, bring out his own gun, but there is nothing he can do because there is nothing left, save for the blackness swallowing him up whole.

CHAPTER THIRTY-ONE

Nolan's Journal

It takes me a long time to drag myself down into the entrance to the old mine. Inside, it is cold but nowhere near as cold as outside. I find a threadbare blanket and wrap it around myself and try to find some slight vestige of sleep.

I wake with a start. With no idea of time, I scramble around, find an old pair of work pants, and, pulling them on, I go outside. The sun is blinding. A new day. Over where they tied me to that tree, there's the body of the man I killed and, about ten paces of so beyond, three scrawny looking buzzards, their eyes on stalks. They have only just begun to tear at the corpse, and they look to me with true hatred for disturbing their breakfast.

Ignoring them, I manage to pick up my clothes and pull them on, gasping as the pain lances through my back. I feel like my back is a single open wound, flesh ripped apart by a giant piece of carpenter's sandpaper. It is difficult for me to ease my arms through the sleeves of the shirt, even worse through a thick coat, some of the scabs on the wounds cracking open, new blood trickling through. If ever I meet up with Shapiro again, I'm gonna take a long time making him pay.

The dead man's gun is lying where I dropped it. I busily put the gun belt around my waist, check the cylinder and drop in fresh cartridges to replace the used ones.

My plan is a simple one – to ride out to Cole's ranch, explain to Julia what I had to do, somehow persuade her that nothing now stands in our way, and make it down to Mexico for a new life. I had toiled with the idea of confusing everyone and going north, way up through Oregon and maybe into Canada. I would see what Julia's opinion is of that. But wherever we end up, I know now that this is where my future lies. She told me that Cole provided her with a home, a roof, somewhere to rest her head, but not a lot else. She had lost so much in her life and I was here to bring some sense of reason to it all. A new start. Perhaps a child, even children.

After I found some stale corn biscuits to munch down, I packed up my horse and rode out. Every step sent a tornado of agony through my back. I knew if I didn't get the lacerations washed and treated, they'd become infected. Perhaps Julia would help. She helped with so much else.

I made good going, despite the pain. A few flurries of snow lapped around my face and I enjoyed the way my skin would cool at their touch. A tiny scratch of worry made itself felt. Perhaps my hot flesh was the first sign of fever. So, I put my head down and kicked my horse into a gallop, trying my best to clear my mind of such nightmare visions.

Some hours later I rein in my horse and gaze down towards the ranch. All seems fine, save for a few more buzzards flying overhead. I put that down to the rank smell coming off my wounds. They must be infected, I reason.

Drawing closer to the little cabin, I see what the true reason is, and I pull up hard.

There is a body. It is black and bloated and the birds are making a meal of him. I ease myself from my horse and draw my pistol. There is no other sound save for the birds squabbling with one another over the choicest pickings.

I give Julia's buggy a half look. The pony is not there but that does not cause me concern. She must have taken it into the nearby barn due to the freezing cold night. The thought reminds me just how low the temperature has plummeted, even during the daylight hours, and I gather my coat around me and edge towards the door.

The smell hits the back of my throat and I gag. I recognise that smell. It is unmistakeable but I force myself to move forward. There is nothing in the little front room, no evidence of any disturbance or anything unusual. I head to the door which leads to the bedroom, the room where we had discovered one another and I stop and stare in disbelief, my world summersaulting into an awful place, filled with pain, anguish and despair.

She is lying on the bed, a blanket over her body, arms like bleached white wooden sticks draped over the top, the flesh of her face a hideous pale green.

Julia. Dead.

I drop to my knees and the tears burst down my cheeks. I cannot hold them back. She is gone and I do not know how. For many moments, perhaps hours, I remain like that, not daring to believe that everything I wanted, everything I *ever* wanted has gone.

Finding the courage, I go to her and take hold of one of those hands, lift it to my lips and kiss. She is so cold. Colder than anything I've endured during my ride or the terrible night in the mine. This is a coldness beyond the living, something one never wishes to experience. Her face, sunken yet still retaining that stark, natural beauty which I so loved, appears peaceful. I sit on the edge of the bed, her hand in mine, and I weep again.

In time, I look at her more deeply. There is a hole in her neck, black, ragged. A bullet hole, but one that somebody has cleaned. Why would someone murder her then lay her down in the bed with such reverence? It makes no sense to me and the more I think about it, the more I simply do not care.

As if in a dream, I leave that ghastly place. I say goodbye to her with a simple kiss on the brow. Ignoring the cold from the snow which now falls much more heavily, I go into the barn. There, sure enough, is the pony, together with the other horses. Acting automatically, without conscious thought, I lead them all to the small paddock, closing the gate, and watch them buck and run. I should feed them, I say to myself, but that task can wait for someone else to do. What I need to do now cannot.

In the barn I find some rope. It does not take long for me to fashion a noose. My years of working in various ranches has taught me well. I no longer care about whoever has ended my life, or why. All I know is that Julia has gone and with her passing all reasons for continuing have also gone. Never to return.

I have taken time to scribble down these last few words in the hope that whoever reads this miserable journal will at least understand what I have done. I have made mistakes and I have so many regrets, but my life has run dry now. Without Julia, there is nothing. Only this final goodbye.

CHAPTER THIRTY-TWO

The End of It

Coles stands in the entrance. He had wondered how the horses had been returned to the paddock and now he knows.

The body swings like a pendulum, the rope creaking with the weight and he remembers the way Captain Fleming's body moved in the same way. No feelings meander through him. He is cold now. As cold as the winter.

After the doc patched Roose up, Cole's old friend insisted coming out to the ranch, so Cole borrowed the Doc's buggy and here they are. Both of them, staring. Cole had shown Roose Julia's body and Roose had wept like a baby. Cole never knew the depths of his old friend's feelings. Another reason for a withdrawal from this world.

"You gonna cut him down?"

Cole looked askance at his old friend. "I'd rather he stayed there and rotted."

"Yeah, but you know you can't do that."

"I guess not."

The silence stretched out between them. Neither moved. Roose swayed, his wounded leg bound and someone, maybe the doc, had given him a walking stick upon which he was leaning. Something on the ground, a thin notebook, the stub of a pencil next to it, grabs his attention. "What's that?"

Cole picked it up and flicked through it. "It's writing. A diary maybe." He looks towards Nolan. "He must have written it."

"Maybe it's a confession?"

"Could be."

They both stare at the body hanging there until at last, Roose sspoke. "So, you gonna cut him down?"

Blowing out a long sigh, Cole's shoulders slump. "We need to bury Julia first."

"Here, at the ranch?"

Cole nods.

More than an hour later they stand before the grave, a simple cross marking the spot. Roose has said some words, but both men know there will never be words enough.

"We'll forget this pain in time," says Roose, replacing his hat, but due to only having one free arm to do so because of the walking stick he leans on, he does not succeed. Reaching across, Cole helps his old friend.

"One day," says Cole.

"Yeah. One day." He lifts his head and stares out across the range. "I'm gonna run for sheriff. My days of scouting are done, Cole. I need to settle, do a job worth doing."

"I reckon that's a good idea, Sterling." Another sigh. So heavy this time, and rattling, as if he is barely able to keep himself under control. "Me too, in a way. I'm retiring, Sterling. No more army for me. There's been too much killing and I'm sick to my stomach of it."

Roose nods. He understands all too well how much these recent events have changed them both. "What will you do with the ranch, after ..." He breaks down again, ramming finger and thumb into his eyes as he does his utmost to control the grief consuming him.

Cole places his arm around his friend and stares at the cross bearing Julia's name. 'Our true love,' it says, 'gone but always here.'

"I'm selling up and moving into Pa's place. He's sick, he needs taking care of. Besides, there is more land there for the stock we have."

Sniffing loudly, Roose drags the back of his free hand across his nose. "Cole, don't you be thinking of doing anything stupid as you rattle around in that big, old house. I don't want you to do what Nolan did."

Cole's face cracks into something akin to a smile. He turns and looks into the distance. Birds are hovering over where the two ex-scouts threw Nolan's corpse. Neither felt they could bury him, so the buzzards have feasted again. "I've always done stupid things, Sterling. But not anymore. I'm done."

Together they look in silence at Julia's grave. Before long, the sun sets beneath the horizon and the air grows chillier than ever, but still they stand and look.

THE END

Dear reader,

We hope you enjoyed reading *Hard Days*. Please take a moment to leave a review, even if it's a short one. Your opinion is important to us.

Discover more books by Stuart G. yates at https://www.nextchapter. pub/authors/stuart-g-yates

Want to know when one of our books is free or discounted? Join the newsletter at http://eepurl.com/bqqB3H

Best regards,

Stuart G. Yates and the Next Chapter Team

You might also like:

No One Can Hide by Stuart G. Yates

To read the first chapter for free, please head to:

https://www.nextchapter.pub/books/no-one-can-hide

Lightning Source UK Ltd.
Milton Keynes UK
UKHW041912031120
372650UK00001BB/251